# HELL'S TEETH
## A DEEP SEA THRILLER

## PAUL MANNERING

SEVERED PRESS
HOBART TASMANIA

# HELL'S TEETH

Copyright © 2016 Paul Mannering
Copyright © 2016 by Severed Press

*WWW.SEVEREDPRESS.COM*

*ISBN: 978-1-925493-67-2*

# CHAPTER 1

Half Moon Bay, Kaikoura Coast, New Zealand. *Latitude: 42° 15' 68" S, Longitude: 173° 48' 27" E*

The northeast wind drove the surf into majestic curves that crashed against the pebble beach. The rocky coast north of the tourist town of Kaikoura on the eastern side of New Zealand's South Island was a mecca for Southern Hemisphere surfers. The Kermadec Trench, an underwater canyon over a mile deep, lay just off shore.

The area was famous as a home to whales and giant squid. The locals had gone from hunting whales in the 1800s to fishing and now whale conservation as they capitalized on the tourists desire to see the incredible creatures.

Dave Halligan paddled out under the darkening sky of the late afternoon. The three-millimeter-thick, full-body wetsuit kept the worst of the chill at bay and the hard exercise of catching waves did the rest. Dave didn't wear a hood or neoprene booties, preferring to feel the sea in his hair and grip the surfboard with his bare toes. The mountains were so close to the coast, as soon as the sun went behind them, it would get much colder. This would be the last surf of the day. After dark, it was easier to go diving, maybe catch some crayfish, the spiny rock lobster that was the other big attraction along this harsh coastline.

Lying flat, Dave paddled through the swell, thankful the wind had been perfect today, curving the waves into great arcs that provided excellent surfing conditions. Each successful ride filled his soul with a contentment he couldn't imagine living without.

When the fin broke the water in front of him, Dave nearly fell off his surfboard. Sharks of different kinds were common in these waters, though attacks on surfers were rare. The surfer stared hard at the fin, and then laughed with relief. Just a dolphin. On those few occasions a shark did attack, the shark had mistaken the surfer for a fur seal. The seals lived in colonies along the rocky coast and the hunting sharks would bite the front end of the surfboard. Which, on a seal, would be a killing blow to the head.

A moment later, the dolphin surfaced and puffed saltwater spray from her blowhole before plunging into the dark face of an oncoming wave.

Dave grinned. *Dolphins, man. The most perfect creatures in the sea. Smart, playful, and a little bit crazy. Just like surfers.* Dropping into the trough between two waves, he sat up and turned his board, ready to paddle like hell to catch the rushing wave. His hands were steady on the front edges of the surfboard, his legs hanging in the water; timing was everything.

As Dave tensed to draw his feet up and go to his knees, prior to standing for the ride, something grey stirred the water under his foot.

"Hey, dolphin buddy," he said, his focus on the wave building behind him. *Now.*

Dave moved into a kneeling position, his hands paddling as he caught the sweet spot on the building wave. Once the board caught the wave, he stood up, adjusting his stance and steering the board along the rising wall. The sheer awesomeness of the ride filled him with joy. Dave moved his feet, twisting the surfboard, riding the plane of the wave as it rose over six feet. With both hands outstretched for balance, Dave flew across the surface, his fingers skimming the breaker, creating a boat-like wake and filling the air with a zipping sound.

When the wide-open jaws snapped closed on his arm above the elbow, Dave only felt a sharp jerking sensation. The force of it pulled him off his board and into the turbulent storm of the breaking wave.

He tried to scream as he saw the black emptiness of a shark's mouth lined with triangular teeth. The water clouded with ink-dark blood and Dave swam for the surface, only then registering that his left arm was gone a few inches below the shoulder.

He screamed with primordial terror and shock, his breath a rising storm of bubbles. The cloud of his own blood, gushing into the cold water, drove the shark into a frenzy. It lunged forward, turning on its back, again baring those unimaginable teeth. The second bite closed around Dave's midsection. The neoprene wetsuit tore as easily as the warm flesh beneath it and the last of the air in Dave's lungs bubbled out from his torn lungs.

As the shark dragged him down into the deeper water, the last things Dave saw were more great white sharks, swimming together and tearing apart the remains of the dolphin.

# CHAPTER 2

Chatham Rise, South Pacific Ocean, *Longitude 44° S, Latitude 176° W*

"You remember Pacman?" Casey asked the newest member of his dive team.

"Uhh, yeah. Kinda... I guess?" The boy looked confused.

Casey made a Pacman jaw shape with his hand. "Great Whites, their tails look like Pacman's mouth. That sharp angle, like a wide open mouth chasing those pills and ghosts."

"Okay." The young diver didn't look sure of where this was going.

"The point is, don't freak out if you see a shark. There's plenty of them out there. Most of them are just doing their own thing. They are more interested in fish than in you. Each species has a unique shape to the tail fins. If it ain't Pacman, it's probably not going to hurt you." Casey smiled reassuringly and moved off to check the rest of the expedition's gear.

At nineteen, Tyler was used to being bullshitted. "Is that true?" he asked Billy, the dive-crew's second-in-command.

"Aww, yeah," the lean Samoan said.

5

"Serious mate, no shit?"

"Way I see it," Billy paused in his careful coiling of ropes, "Shark comes at you, you get your knife out and stab that fella in the nose."

Tyler nodded. It was what he had always understood. A shark's nose was sensitive; a good thump would send one scurrying off in search of easier prey.

"Of course, you have to get close enough to that bloody shark to let you punch him, eh?" Billy grinned, his teeth white against the brown of his skin.

Tyler felt less certain than ever. This far south, the Pacific Ocean was cold and grey. The nearest land was the tiny archipelago of the Chatham Islands, 420 miles off the east coast of New Zealand's South Island. They were halfway there, a small ship alone in a vast desert.

"Go ask those university fellas, eh?" Billy suggested.

Tyler looked up the deck towards the bow of the ship. The addition of a marine biology team to the expedition was a nice treat, especially when it turned out the team included two girls. It was a bit weird to Tyler that one of the girls was in charge. She'd been introduced as Aroha Halligan, *Doctor* Aroha Halligan. Tyler reckoned that meant she'd paid a lot more attention in school than Tyler ever did.

"Hey, isn't it bad luck to have women on ships?" Tyler asked.

The Samoan threw back his head and laughed. "Only if they don't like you, mate."

Tyler hoped Aroha liked him. With her bleached hair, tanned skin, and fit physique, she didn't look like a book nerd. Tyler laughed with Billy and helped him stow the ropes in the on-deck cabinet.

*

"I can't believe they are seriously doing this," Nari Prasad, the second woman on the science team said to Aroha. In their mid-twenties, they were close in age and freshly graduated with doctorates in their fields of study. For Nari, it was low-oxygen marine environments and for Aroha, it was great white sharks. Though entire libraries of research existed libraries about the most feared of the ocean predators, the Pacific waters off New Zealand's east coast were a hotspot for the most famous shark species. In these cold southern waters, they had exhibited behavior unseen in other populations and a lot was still unknown about the life cycle of these incredible creatures.

"It's okay, Nari." Aroha was focused on the rugged laptop in front of her as the ship rose and fell with the ocean swell.

"Any kind of mineral exploration is going to cause untold devastation to the environment," Nari continued. "Taking samples is only going to encourage them."

Nari's research into the strange habitats found in the deepest parts of the ocean had shown indicators of rich phosphate and more precious mineral deposits in the silt and mud. The mineral prospecting companies jumped on the data as they sought virgin land to exploit for resources and profit.

"They are paying enough for us to conduct research for a year, Nari. Besides, if the mining companies weren't footing the bill, we would both be sitting on the mainland, marking undergrad papers."

Nari shuddered; the only thing she loathed more than corporate mining's disregard for the natural environment was working with students.

"If they so much as knock over a chimney..." Nari warned. The hydrothermal vents provided a unique alien environment for many forms of life in the dark depths and mineral-rich chimneys formed around the hot water rushing out of the earth's depths.

"Wasn't it you who told me those chimneys can grow at up to thirty centimeters a day?" Aroha teased her friend.

The Indian scientist bit back her sharp reply as the deck door opened and Casey, the leader of the commercial diver team, came inside.

"We're all set," Casey announced.

Aroha nodded, a blush rising on her neck, as she went back to staring at her computer screen. Two days out of port and she still couldn't look Casey in the eye. *I am never drinking again*, Aroha reminded herself.

"I'm heading up to the bridge," Casey said. His fair hair and unshaven face stood out in high-contrast against the wind-burned tan of his skin. "If you want to come, Doc."

"Sure," Nari grinned, "I'll come. What about you, Doctor Halligan?" she asked.

"No, that's fine. Go on without me," Aroha muttered, staring at the weather report on the screen as if her life depended on it.

Nari followed Casey up the internal stairs. The *Waitangirua* was a commercial diving vessel with a crew of ten and room for supplies, gear storage, and space for two mini-subs on deck.

The ship's captain, Vincent "Mac" Macquarie, smoked

constantly. His fingers were stained with nicotine and calloused from sixty years of hard labor on ships of all sizes and types. Mac glanced at the new arrivals as they emerged from the staircase and smoke jetted from his nostrils.

"What?" he asked, barely moving lips around the flickering tip of his hand-rolled cigarette.

Casey spoke up. "All set, Captain. Just waiting for you to put us on the right spot."

Mac grunted and jetted smoke again. "Got you right on the money," he said. A gnarled finger jabbed at the various glowing screens in front of him. "All engines stop," he ordered.

"All engines stop," Kelly, the ship's first mate, replied as she eased the throttle back on the console. The drone of the ship's engines reduced to an idling purr.

"What's the depth?" Nari whispered, hardly daring to speak up in front of the gruff captain.

"Four hundred meters. That's over thirteen hundred feet," Mac replied. His hearing was sharp as his navigation skills. "Anchor it," he snarled.

"Anchors away," Kelly replied. The hull vibrated as anchors fore and aft plunged into the water and began their rush to the distant bottom.

"You'd best get on with it," Mac ordered without looking at Casey or Nari.

"Roger that." Casey followed Nari down the stairs as the ship rose and fell in the gentle swell.

In the room below the bridge, the divers and science team had gathered and Casey brought them up to speed.

"We are on site," he announced. "The habitat was finished last month and one of our team will go down first to ensure that everything is still working. I know you have trained for this and you are all experienced divers, but, I will say this again, where we are going is nothing like your usual SCUBA trip to look at the pretty fish. At four hundred meters, it is dark and cold and the pressure is a fuck of a lot higher than you can imagine.

"This is a saturation dive. Which means you can look forward to a couple of days in a decompression chamber when you get back. We'll be taking you down in the dive bell and you need to obey every single instruction given to you by the dive team and alert us immediately if you find yourself in difficulty."

He looked around the group; three divers and seven civilians in all, two women and five men, including an underwater video specialist, his two video production assistants, a geologist, and a deep-sea mining engineer. The last two would be earning their keep, taking core samples and determining if it was worth committing company resources to a full drilling expedition. The cost of a prospecting mission with equipment like that would be high even without all the lobbying and bureaucratic rigmarole to jump through to get the necessary permits and licenses.

The video crew were mining company men, with experience working on offshore drilling platforms, tropical jungles, and deserts. How they got into a soft job like camera operating and editing was a mystery to Casey. The three of them looked like hard bastards. Not that it mattered a damn where they were going. Casey knew from experience that even the toughest could break when they went deep.

"There will be two trips. First, Steve and Billy will take Doctor Prasad, Doctor Halligan, Doctor Steele, and Mister Hudson. Then I'll bring the video crew and their gear."

Steele, the geologist, had the tanned and wiry frame of a field scientist. Only his salt-and-pepper beard suggested he was close to retirement age and still he grinned like a kid on Christmas morning. Behind his TV screen-sized glasses, his eyes sparkled with delight.

Hudson, the deep-sea engineer, was half Steele's age and his face had the solemnity of a judge. Casey had worked with him before on other projects and knew that Hudson's reputation for being the best man for the job was justified.

Casey closed his briefing. "Any questions? Okay then, use the bathroom; trust me, it'll be a few days before you get to go comfortably again. Steve will help you with your dive gear and complete the safety checks. I'll see you all on the bottom."

The room cleared in silence, until only Casey and Aroha remained.

"You okay?" he asked.

"I'm fine."

"You don't have to do this. If you're not ready, I mean. We can bring you down later."

Aroha looked at him for the first time. "I said, I'm fine."

Casey wanted to say he was sorry about her brother. The news had reached them in port two days before they shipped out. Aroha's brother, Dave, was killed in a shark attack while surfing off the Kaikoura coast.

Aroha had been understandably shocked and devastated; it

was in support of her that Casey took her drinking the night before they boarded the *Waitangirua* and left the port of Lyttelton. Ending up in bed together hadn't been what either of them intended, and since then, Aroha found it hard to make eye-contact.

Casey nodded and walked out to the deck, inhaling the fresh air. The motion of the boat always made him nauseous and on the surface, he felt close to drowning. Underwater, those fears vanished, and he was completely calm and focused; he missed that tranquility when he was onshore.

"First group should be ready in a few minutes," he announced.

"Yeah, boss," Billy replied without looking up from doing the technical checks on Tyler's gear.

The young diver stood next to a large suit of armor that weighed over 500 pounds and looked like a tire company mascot. The steel and fiberglass suit protected a diver to a depth of a thousand feet.

Casey frowned for a moment. "I'll go start the monitoring and comms system check."

Tyler watched Casey walking away from the corner of his eye. "I could totally drive the bell."

"Uh-huh," Billy grunted.

"Seriously, man. Casey should let me take it."

"Didn't you crash his truck?" Billy paused and looked at Tyler.

"I barely scratched it."

"You backed his truck into a concrete wall and you expect

him to let you drive the bell with passengers?"

"I—"

"No." Billy opened the gleaming armored suit. "You ready to get canned?"

"Like a sardine." Tyler pushed his arms into the stiff molded arm sections and settled his feet into the heavy boots.

"Air okay?" Billy asked.

Tyler felt the flow of cold gas coming into the suit caress his face. "Yeah."

Billy closed the suit from behind and sealed the sections.

*"You on the air yet?"* Casey's voice echoed in the fish-bowl helmet.

"Comm's check," Tyler said into the helmet microphone.

*"Comm's check confirmed,"* Casey replied. *"What are you going to do?"*

Tyler rolled his eyes. "I'm going to descend on the umbilical line to a depth of two-hundred and seventy meters."

*"And then?"*

"Hold until the cargo passes and Steve brings the bell back up."

*"Nothing else,"* Casey warned.

"The suit can go to three hundred meters easy," Tyler said.

*"Yes, it can. But you aren't going that deep."*

"I could drive the bell, which would give me more certified dive hours."

*"I haven't forgotten what you did to my truck."*

"Yes, Dad," Tyler muttered.

*"Hey, you are only here because your father asked me to help*

*out with getting you more commercial dive experience. So watch the attitude."*

"Roger that. All suit systems green. Ready to launch."

Tyler had been diving since he was a kid. Finally old enough to get his commercial diving certificates and then breaking into the insular world of commercial diving had been a dream come true. It had only been possible due to his father's connections as a maintenance engineer on ships and underwater pipelines. Casey was taking him on this job as a favor to Tyler's old man, and there was no way the boy was going to screw it up.

*"You hear me, bro?"* Billy's voice came on the line.

"Loud and clear."

"Taking you up now," Billy replied. A moment later, the heavy suit creaked, as the steel cable attached to a hydraulic crane arm took the weight and lifted Tyler off the deck.

With careful precision on the crane's controls, Billy maneuvered the suit off the deck and over the open water. Tyler's teeth tingled at the vibration from the winch motor as the metal frame descended. He slipped into the water and focused on breathing steadily. The waves rose and fell and then he was underwater and at the mercy of the currents.

*"You secured yet?"* Casey's voice growled in his ear.

"Hang on, Jesus…" Tyler felt more confident now he was in the water and out of the direct gaze of the dive leader. He hung suspended by the crane cable in water with a visible range of about twenty feet, not bad for this part of the world. Even the halogen lights built into his suit couldn't penetrate much further.

Activating the inbuilt propellers, Tyler turned the suit through ninety degrees. The bundle of air, power, and communication's cables that went to the habitat on the bottom hung like a thick jungle vine in front of him. On the surface, the cable remained secured to an anchored platform with a flashing light and a beeping radio transmitter to warn any passing boats of the hazard. The lines passed from the platform to the ship where the generators and compressor pumps hummed and whirred.

Tyler attached a thin wire cable attached to an auto-braking descender from the armored suit to a thicker steel rope marked with an orange flag that indicated it was for equipment connections. He locked the descender on the cable; it would be strong enough to hold the suit in position until Tyler released the grip.

"I am secured and ready to descend." Tyler felt a rush of adrenaline. He could see his feet, the white-painted metal boots almost glowing against the dark backdrop. It was a long way down and shit was about to get real.

*"Hold your horses."* Casey could have been standing next to him given the clarity of the transmission. This time, Tyler kept his mouth shut; the communications link was always open, and it wasn't too late for Casey to drag his ass out of the adventure.

At the other end of the taut cable, four hundred meters down in on the cold silt, the habitat set up for the team of divers and explorers waited in the dark. The habitat was a modular construction that made for a cramped shelter with air recycling, a mechanical toilet, and little in the way of comfort or luxuries. It would keep the team safe and dry for the two days they would spend completing their survey of the seafloor.

"Can I disconnect from the ship-line?" Tyler asked. The swirling currents this close to the surface were pushing him around like seaweed in the tide.

"*No.*" Casey didn't elaborate and Tyler resigned himself to hanging like a kid on a swing until Casey gave the order for him to disconnect.

With his air supply coming from the surface, Tyler would spend his entire trip at normal pressure, protected by the strength of the suit from the high pressure of an ocean of water pressing in on him and dissolving gas into his blood.

The divers in the bell were going to be out and exploring in the depths. That meant they were already breathing a cocktail of nitrogen, helium, and oxygen, called Trimix; it was the safest breathing gas mixture for deep diving.

*

The dive bell slipped into the water twenty minutes later. Tyler stirred and blinked away the boredom that had set in long ago.

"We're in the water," Billy said into the headset. Steve, the other member of Casey's dive crew, checked readouts and confirmed everything was in the green. Behind the two pilots, four civilians sat pressed into the curved bench seats of the diving bell. Trimix air tanks and dive gear took up the rest of the interior of the steel sphere that would deliver them to the bottom in relative comfort and safety.

"*Dive bell is ready to descend,*" Steve said.

"*Dive bell, you are cleared for descent.*"

"*Initiating dive bell descent,*" Steve replied. Tyler watched as the gleaming yellow sphere slipped down into the darkness. A thousand facts about the dangers of diving were always lurking in the back of Tyler's mind. His dad had been a careful diver, enforcing rules that Tyler never took for granted. Diving to this depth had its own special risks, which is why Tyler waited unmoving, staring into the darkness below.

*"Tyler, disconnect the ship line and follow them down. And watch your depth gauge."* Casey could have been ordering a pizza for all the emotion in his voice.

Tyler unclipped the line that had lowered him from the ship's deck, took a final breath, and let himself follow the dive bell into the dark.

# CHAPTER 3

Chatham Rise, South Pacific Ocean, *Longitude 44° S, Latitude 176° W.*

"Two hundred and seventy meters," Tyler said into the bubble-like shell of his dive suit. The dive computer on his wrist glowed with a green luminescence as the digital read out ticked over the numbers.

This was well beyond where the amateur divers stopped. Below 60 meters, there were no pretty fish and even less light. Deeper than 100 meters, the desert really started. At that depth, you were in the outer space of the seas, a vast empty expanse of ocean between where the light-loving plants and animals lived, and the cold, dark silt of the bottom where sea monsters lived in eternal darkness and crushing pressure.

At this depth, most creatures were passing through; whales diving for squid, sharks and other creatures traversing the thermoclines in the constant search for food and sex.

*"Tyler, hold your position. Lock onto the safety line."* Casey's voice in Tyler's ear made him feel like an astronaut on a

spacewalk, a human floating in an alien and deadly space, protected only by his suit and sustained by his air-supply.

"Securing the line." Tyler kept breathing in a slow and steady rhythm. Using a metal pincer extending from the wrist stump of the metal suit, he locked the descender brake. Now all Tyler had to do was stand here and wait in the dark for a couple of hours until the dive bell returned to the surface on its final trip. Then he would ride up with it and spend the next couple of days wishing he were on the bottom with everyone else.

"Line secured, I think I'll take a nap," Tyler transmitted.

"*If I hear snoring, you're fired,*" Casey replied.

In the crowded dive bell, the radio conversation sounded thin and tinny coming from the small speaker mounted in the control console.

"Three hundred and fifty meters," Billy said into his headset microphone.

"*Let us know when you see the bottom. The habitat power systems should be running,*" Casey replied.

"Everyone okay?" Billy asked. They all nodded, faces alert and excited with just a hint of terror. "Pressure will increase as we descend. Your body will adapt. Once we are on the bottom, you can go across to the habitat."

Charlie spoke up, his voice betraying the nervousness behind his confidence. "Being on the bottom is okay. Your body will balance the pressure of the water with internal pressure. The trick is surfacing. If we come up too fast, your body's internal pressure will not have time to depressurize and you will rupture pretty much all your cells."

Billy turned his head and gave a warm smile. "It's not that bad, eh? You just gotta go into decompression when we surface. The dive bell seals on the way up. The ship winches it on board and connects us to the decompression chamber. Couple of days, you'll be sweet as."

Staring out through the nearest thick porthole window, Aroha watched the swirling mist of floating particulates; it seemed like there might be a light coming up from below.

"Coming up on the habitat now," Billy reported and they watched the glow become brighter and less diffused as the dive bell got closer. Nari leaned forward, her nose touching the round window. She almost jerked out of her seat when a long shadow swam through the light.

"Sheep!" she squeaked.

"You okay?" Steve asked immediately.

"Yeah, just a fish." Nari winced and avoided eye contact with Jessie, who sat across from her and was trying not to grin at Nari's way of turning regular words into cussing.

"Keep cool," Billy said with no trace of mockery in his voice. "Three hundred and eighty meters, I can see the hab. Eighty-five... ninety... ninety-five... lock the winch."

The wire rope took the strain and the bell swayed slightly as they came to a halt.

"We're here," Billy said.

"How's the habitat?" Casey's voice crackled.

"Looks good." Arthur Steele, the weathered geologist, grinned as he wiped condensation from his glasses and went back to staring out the small window.

# CHAPTER 4

Chatham Rise, South Pacific Ocean, *Longitude 44° S, Latitude 176° W.*

A puff of silt curled around Billy's feet. The heavy boots he wore on his feet allowed him to walk around easily. The heavy commercial diving helmet he wore included halogen lamps and a radio communications system that could reach the dive bell's transceiver. From there, the signal went up the wire to the ship.

"I'm on the bottom. The hab is right next to me."

*"Keep an eye out for descending cargo."* Casey's voice came in a distorted echo.

Now the ship would send down the sealed containers of gear and supplies that weren't already in the habitat. Billy's first job was to make sure everything landed safely and disconnect the dive bags that would act as parachutes for the boxes. A carabineer connected each crate to the cable line.

*"First crate is coming down, descent rate around forty meters a minute,"* Casey reported.

*Great,* Billy thought. *That's ten minutes for me to get these folks inside.* He let his gaze wander over the spherical compartments of the habitat. Made from an aluminum frame, overlaid with carbon fiber and fiberglass in a similar technique to his helmet, the habitat had a pressure rating to a depth of a thousand meters. Realistically though, anyone working at that depth would be inside a submersible and wouldn't be staying longer than the course of one dive.

The undersea shelter had a cloverleaf shape made up of six capsules clipped onto a central column. At the top of the column was a seventh sphere. This held the communications array and emergency gear. In an emergency, the seventh sphere could be sealed and disconnected from the rest of the habitat, allowing the dive team to surface and then the entire capsule would be winched onto the deck of the support ship and attached to a decompression chamber so the occupants' bodies could slowly return to surface pressure. The interior of the return pod was cramped, but the habitat had space for ten crew for as long as they had contact with a surface supply ship.

*

"*First cargo is at one hundred meters,*" Casey reported.

"Roger that." Tyler looked upwards, no sign of the crate yet. *Give it a minute,* he reminded himself.

The shadow that passed through the beam of his headlamp was unmistakable; the sinuous grace of a shark passing overhead. Tyler barely breathed as he watched the predator vanish into the gloom. *Thirteen feet long, at least.* In his fright, he had forgotten to try to see the shape of the tail.

Tyler let out a slow breath as a second shark swam into view, almost as large as the first one. Then another.

Within a minute, five sharks had casually circled the cable before vanishing into the darkness.

Tyler stared down into the abyss, feeling a crushing sense of scale and isolation pressing in on him with the weight of eternity.

"*Three hundred and fifty meters,*" Casey said in Tyler's ear. "*Can you see it?*"

"Roger," Tyler replied. The bright plastic of the descending crate was visible now, the netting around it creating a dark lattice.

The shark charged from the darkness with singular focus at a terrifying speed. Its mouth gaped wide as the body twisted. The soft bag of air controlling the crate's descent vanished into the shark's mouth and tore in a burst of bubbles. The crate plummeted. Tyler flailed his arms as he tried to maneuver backwards. "Shit!" he yelped as the crate whooshed passed him.

"*What?*" Casey barked immediately.

"Fucking shark! A fucking big shark just came in and tore the bag off a crate. Nearly dropped it on my head!"

"*Is the crate okay?*" Casey asked.

Tyler calmed his breathing. The ragged gasps were a gateway to panic and panic would get you killed down here.

"It was moving pretty fast. Billy, watch your head."

"*I hear ya,*" Billy's voice came through the relay of comms cables.

"*Crate's here. Hang on... I'll check it out.*" Billy moved forward, his feet raising puffs of grey silt. The crate had come to rest on the bottom with a jolt, but it seemed otherwise intact.

"*Crate's okay. I think Tyler shit himself, though,*" Billy reported.

Casey almost chuckled. "*I'll lay out a clean pair of undies on his cot before I come down. Tyler, keep an eye out for the next crate and if you see any sharks, tell them to piss off.*"

Tyler grinned; Casey's voice was calm and reassuring. Just another story to tell when they got home.

The shark vanished into the dark, leaving Tyler shaken but alone.

\*

When the last of the crates touched down, Billy reported their safe arrival up the line. He walked back to the dive bell. "Steve?" he said into his mic.

"*Swimmers are all geared up and ready to leave the bell,*" Steve said.

"Divers, can you hear me?"

"*Ah, yeah, can you hear us? Uhm, over?*" Aroha sounded nervous, but excited.

"I hear you loud and clear. If everyone is ready, then come down through the bottom of the bell, one at a time."

Charlie Hudson, the engineer, slipped into the water, feet first, arms extended in the cold water as he sank the last few meters to the dark silt of the bottom. Billy stood waiting with his arms folded across his chest like a genie fresh from the bottle. Aroha and Nari slid into the water next, long streams of exhaled bubbles rising to the surface. The two scientists had SCUBA diving certificates and experience, but this descent into the abyssal dark thirteen hundred feet below the surface required specialist training. Putting those freshly learned skills into practice had them both feeling excited and terrified.

*"Everyone okay?"* Steve asked over the radio. Nari gave Billy the thumbs up and grinned wide enough to be seen around the silicone mask.

*"All okay,"* Billy transmitted. He would have to remind the women that in diving terminology a thumbs up meant you needed to surface.

Arthur was the last of the civilian divers to join them. His eyes crinkled with delight. *"It's like walking on an alien world."*

*"This is great,"* Aroha said, turning slowly and peering into the gloom.

*"It's a different world,"* Nari said, her hands waving slowly as she turned to stare at the dark seabed.

The pressure had built steadily as they went down; now, outside the protection of the dive bell, Aroha and Nari felt the water pressing in around them like a vice.

Billy kept an eye on the water. He also watched the other four divers, his dive computer, the habitat, the dive bell, and its thick lines of cables that rose to the surface.

*"Look out for the sharks, eh?"* Tyler's voice came through the relay of cables and radio transmitters.

Billy wished he wouldn't say things like that. There was no reason to get people nervous. Sharks were harmless, unless you were a fish. "If you will all follow me, we will get you into the habitat."

The civilian divers formed an orderly line, and Billy escorted them the twenty meters across the ocean floor to the habitat.

"You'll only be in there for a couple of days. You'll be so busy you won't notice how cramped the habitat is, or how bad you smell," Billy said, the humor evident in his tone.

*"Can we go inside now?"* Aroha asked.

Two hundred and thirty meters above the divers, Tyler wanted to say something cool, like, *Me Casa, Su Casa.* By the time he thought of it, it would be weird, so he kept his mouth shut.

The divers ducked under the struts buried in the silt and walked to the dive portal under the central column. A short ladder extended down, making it easy to climb inside the pressurized environment and finally stop breathing from the tanks on their backs.

Billy climbed up and helped the others out of the supporting density of the water. The weight of the gear they wore dragged on them, and they shrugged out of their BCD's and heavy gas tanks with audible sighs of relief.

Billy kept his gear on. "Hey, Charlie, can you give me a hand getting the crates in, mate?"

Charlie nodded, his face impassive. He tightened the straps on his BCD and slipped his helmet back on. Taking a deep breath through his respirator, he gave Billy an OK hand signal.

"The rest of you, go through that door. You'll find towels and stuff to make a hot drink. We'll be back in a minute."

The Samoan climbed down the ladder, sinking out of sight and leaving a stream of bubbles in his wake.

Outside the habitat, Billy retrieved a chemical glow stick from his vest, bent it until the glass vial inside cracked, and then gave it a vigorous shake. The chemical reaction emitted a bright red luminescence that turned most colors down here to a washed-out pink.

Charlie joined him a moment later, and they walked across the silt to where the net-bound crates had touched down. Working together, the two divers released the last of the air from the bright parachutes. Each squeeze of the heavy plastic sent large bubbles boiling upwards. Folding the yellow sheets, they tucked them securely into the netting.

*"Hey."* Charlie jerked his head up and pointed towards the dive bell. Billy turned as fast as he could in his heavy drysuit.

The cluster of cables rising above the dive bell went slack and started to drop. Weighing in at around a pound per foot, the line coiled as it fell, and over 1000 pounds of copper and high-density rubber tumbled out of the dark water overhead.

Billy started forward, but Charlie grabbed his arm and yanked him backwards.

"Steve! Stay in the bell!" Billy yelled. With the communications cable coming down around them, his transmission went nowhere.

With the loss of the lines holding the dive bell, it started to tilt. With the change in angle, the pressure changed and seawater exploded up through the open base of the metal chamber.

Charlie and Billy could only stare helpless, as Steve's shocked face swept across the porthole view and the foaming water smashed him into the steel walls.

# CHAPTER 5

*Chatham Rise. South Pacific Ocean, Longitude 44° S, Latitude 176° W. Commercial dive vessel: Waitangirua*

Casey had sat hunched over the dive control and monitoring station for the past hour. The computer screens in front of him communicated data via a clip-on unit attached to the dive computer connected to each crewmember's BCD. After watching Tyler like a hawk, Casey decided that the kid might be okay. He took his job seriously and kept his breathing under control even when things got tense.

The hand-held radio on the narrow table beside him squawked. "Yeah?" Casey replied into it.

"*Docs are ready to go,*" Billy said.

"Take 'em down, Billy. I'll bring the rest of the team once you are on the bottom."

"*No worries.*" The camera view from inside the dive bell came online and showed him the people inside were making a smooth descent to into the dark abyss.

\*

"Get back!" Billy ordered. The comms units worked wirelessly over a short-range, but for communication to the surface, they needed the wired connection in the cable that was now piling up on the silt around them.

Charlie hesitated, transfixed by the coiling line crashing down. High above, the water flashed with lightning in streaks of orange and yellow. Seconds later, a massive shockwave of bubbles sent a mass of twisted metal chunks and debris tumbling downwards.

Billy charged forward, crashing into Charlie. The impact sent the other man sprawling backwards as an L-shaped piece of steel, at least twenty feet long and weighing a ton, slammed into the silt behind them. Billy let out a grunt, and stood, almost floating over the engineer as the storm of disturbed silt engulfed them.

The wave of expanding pressure rippled through the water. Unable to compress the liquid, the explosion travelled like a hurricane wind and threw everything in its path spinning into chaos.

Charlie's view vanished in a cloud of dark silt. His first instinct was to rise to the surface, to get back to the ship and to breathe fresh air. The panic that surged through him made his fingers numb. He scrambled for the inflator valve on his buoyancy compensator.

The ocean around him roared as if he had plunged over a waterfall and was now at the mercy of gravity and the raging current. More flashes, and a rolling boom of thunder pitched low and slow by the pressure of the cold water washed over him. The noise vibrated Charlie's internal organs and he struggled to keep his nausea in check.

The third explosion sent him rolling over the soft silt of the seabed. Charlie saw flickering lights and a rain of falling debris. It seemed the entire world was coming down on his head in spiraling stars of shattered steel.

*

Casey ignored the shouting; on a ship like this one, someone was always yelling. When the first gunshot sounded, he lifted his head and yanked the headphones down to his neck.

*What the hell?* He listened hard. More shouts and then the staccato hammering of automatic weapons fire. Such weapons were strictly illegal in New Zealand and the waters around the country. The sound filled Casey with cold dread.

When the door handle twisted and the recessed steel door burst open, Casey had vanished. The laughing faces of the oil company cinematographer and his assistant had changed to hard expressions of cold determination as they looked around for anywhere the dive leader could have taken refuge.

The muzzles of their SMGs swept the room, ready to fire at the slightest sign of threat.

"Clear, Vlok" the leaner of the two announced. His South African accent was quite different from the Irish brogue he had spoken previously.

"Three minutes," Vlok, the heavier of the two, said, glancing at the watch on his wrist. "Find Carl," he continued.

"Make sure the charges are set." Vlok's accent had changed, too. The working class London English of it now strongly

Afrikaans.

The second gunman nodded and stepped out of the room.

"You in here, mate?" the remaining South African asked. "There's nowhere you can fuckin' hide. You best come out and get this over with." He stepped further into the dimly lit room. On the narrow desk, the computer screens still showed the steady descent of the dive team. The South African ducked and peered under the furniture, finding no sign of his elusive prey.

"It's nothing personal mate," Vlok said. "There's people out there who take the environment very seriously is all. They pay bloody well, too. Me, I don't give a shit. You can mine every strip of sand there is for all I care. But, these fellas, they want to send a message. And in this case, that means shootin' the bloody messenger." Vlok almost laughed at his own joke.

Casey's muscles screamed and his palms started to sweat as he pressed himself against the steel beams of the ceiling. The room was only eight feet from floor to roof and the un-insulated frame wore a thick coat of protective cream paint that felt slick under his damp hands.

The assassins had only missed him by sheer luck in the gloom. Casey let go and dropped, belly-flop style, straight onto the bigger man's shoulders. His fists crashed down on the man's neck and drove him to the floor. The diver had never fired anything more than a hunting rifle in his life. He swept the automatic weapon aside, sending it skating across the floor and sliding under a cabinet as he grappled with the gunman.

Vlok writhed like a snake, his body twisting under Casey and throwing him clear. Casey rolled to his feet and bolted for the room's only exit. The man behind him was some kind of mercenary terrorist, which meant he probably knew how to kill people with his bare hands.

The narrow corridor that ran the length of the lower deck felt like the inside of a narrow train carriage. Casey sprinted towards the stairs, the skin between his shoulder blades writhing in anticipation of a killing blow. Bounding up the stairs, Casey threw open the door that led outside. The wind had picked up, and dark clouds were forming on the southern horizon, a clear indication of bad weather coming in off the Antarctic ice.

Ahead of the approaching storm, a ship could be seen, similar in size to the *Waitangirua* and bearing down on them. Casey felt a flood of relief. It might be a naval ship, or even a fishing trawler responding to a distress call Mac had made.

The diver headed up the outer stairs, approaching the bridge from the rear.

Tommo, one of the ship's crew, lay in a spreading pool of his own blood on the metal landing. His corpse blocked access to the wheelhouse. Casey ducked down as he heard a shout from below. The South African he had tackled earlier came out on to the back deck and yelled at another armed man who emerged through a hatch in the rear.

*{Did you see where that bastard went?}* *"Het jy gesien waar daai donner heen verdwyn het?"*

*{Which one?}* *"Watter een?"* the second man said, his SMG pointed skywards.

*{The bloody diver.}* *"Die donnerse duiker."*

*{No, but the crew's been taken care of.}* *"Nee, maar die*

*bemanning is na gesien."*

*{Good. Now find that fucker. I'm going to gut him.}* "Goed so. Kry nou daai fokker. Ek gaan sy derms uitsny."

Casey crawled on his belly to the edge of the wheelhouse landing and around the corner. The narrow walkway here circled the bridge and gave him a place to remain unseen unless they came up and looked.

The wide windows of the bridge had shattered in a hail of bullets. Casey could see splashes of blood on the walls and he hoped that Mac had gone down fighting.

The second ship rose and fell on the building swell a hundred feet from the *Waitangirua*. The armed men below Casey didn't seem concerned about the anonymous ship's presence. After a moment, figures appeared on deck, and an inflatable Zodiac boat lowered into the surging water.

"Vlok?!" a man with grey hair and a beard yelled from the small boat as it rode the sea between the two ships.

The South African went to the rail and peered over the side. "Hold your fuckin' horses, man!" he yelled.

Vlok's team secured a rope ladder and lowered it over the side. Casey watched as the grey-haired man and a younger woman climbed on to the ship.

"Is it done?" the grey-haired man asked, his accent American.

"Of course. You hired me to do the bloody job, it's bloody done," Vlok snapped.

"Good man. The bombs in place?"

"*Jah*. The timer starts when I click this." Vlok lifted a khaki-green plastic handle from his pocket.

"Outstanding, man." The grey-haired man beamed. "We have to make a statement that they will hear around the world."

"Sure." Vlok looked neither impressed nor interested in what the older man was saying.

Two more gunmen converged on the three of them. Casey recognized them as the technical assistants on the video crew. Company men, he had assumed. Sent here to document and record the findings of the science team. Someone was going to be in deep shit when they learned their contractors were in fact South African mercenaries working for some old nutter.

"Let's go," Vlok ordered. The armed men went over the side with the practiced ease of professional soldiers. The grey-haired man and the silent woman went next. Vlok climbed over the rail and then paused, his cold blue eyes sweeping the deck one last time.

"You hear me fucker?!" Vlok called out. "You've got maybe five minutes to get off this ship before it goes down. You and your friends are dead! Fish are gonna eat your fuckin' eyeballs!" Satisfied that he had the last word, Vlok went down the ladder, and a moment later, the Zodiac buzzed away from the condemned ship.

Casey sprang to his feet and made his way to the deck. The inflatable lifeboats hung in ragged tatters of heavy florescent plastic from their cabinets. Even the flare guns and ammunition were missing. Fear gripped Casey as he ran to the first of the ship's two exploration submersibles. He peered through the thick Perspex windshield and narrowed his eyes. Resting on the narrow pilot's seat was an orange plastic case, about the size of a

lunchbox with a red digital readout counting down, *00:00:07…*
*00:00:06…*

*"Shit!"* Casey ran for it. The reinforced steel of the sub's hull contained the explosion, but the interior controls and systems disintegrated in a storm of compressed fire and pure oxygen. If Vlok was right, then there were other devices on the ship; enough to scuttle the boat right out from under him. Casey weighed up his choices. He could try to get to the communications room and send out a mayday. If Vlok's men hadn't destroyed the radios, then they weren't as smart as they looked.

After an agonizing moment of indecision, Casey headed for the dive locker. He suited up in record time. An internal voice was counting down, *how long?* Five minutes Vlok had said. *What if he was lying? How long had it been? Three minutes? Four?*

Casey strapped on the Trimix air-tanks and BCD. The movements were automatic, the same sequence had been through thousands of times, each step important for safety and efficiency. Clips clicked and zippers ran. He grabbed a pair of fins and a heavy-duty torch from the cabinet and ran for the dive platform. The hydraulic arm and metal grille at the end were designed to raise and lower divers from the surface to the deck. With the weight of all his gear on, and no one to help work the controls, Casey worked fast.

The platform winch moved with agonizing slowness away from the ship. Casey left it running and ran. Taking an oversized step, he grabbed the winch line and felt the metal platform rattle and sway under his feet. With one hand gripping the metal cable, he worked his neoprene boots into the fins. With his mask and respirator in position, he took a breath of Trimix. *All good.*

It would be a long drop to the water from here, but he could do it. Better than staying—

The ship shuddered and the water boiled in a sudden froth of released energy. Under the surface, lightning flashed and the ship groaned as steel tore open under the assault of the demolition charges.

Everything tilted and Casey grabbed on to the steel rope with both hands. The stricken ship pitched over to the port side. In high seas, it could right itself from such an angle, but as the cold ocean water poured in through the torn hull, the ship rolled further and started to sink.

Casey's feet slid off the platform as everything turned on its side and he hung over empty space. Below him, the side of the ship shuddered and swayed. What had been the starboard side of the ship was now pointing towards the sky. The winch frame swung like a pendulum and ripped the cable out of the pulley system as the unexpected angle took the fittings beyond their tolerances.

*Fuck!* Under his fins, the ocean boiled and the ship started dropping fast. A door had broken away under the explosive pressure of rising water and compressed air. Directly below Casey, the dark doorway churned with floating debris and surging seawater.

*Hang on...* he told himself. Once the ship sank, he could let go of the winch cable and swim for his life. *Just a few more seconds.*

The crane arm gave way as the deck plate buckled and the bolts sheared off. The jarring shock shook Casey off the line, and he barely had time to cross his arms and make his body as straight as possible before he dropped into the maelstrom of the sinking ship.

# CHAPTER 6

*Chatham Rise, South Pacific Ocean, Longitude 44° S, Latitude 176° W. 400 meters below the surface.*

When the lightning flash of the explosions hit Tyler, he thought it must be one of the submarines coming down. Holding on to the safety line, he tilted the heavy dive suit back and stared up to the surface.

A moment later, the shockwave hit, sending Tyler tumbling deeper, the safety lines collapsed around him.

"Casey!" he called. "What's going on?"

He heard nothing but static in reply. The cables that secured the dive bell and his communications lines wrapped around the rigid dive-suit and the added weight pushed Tyler into the depths faster.

The suit had been made to dive deeper than any regular drysuit. The increasing pressure of rapid descent would cause all kinds of problems if he was not protected in a ceramic and steel shell. *What happens when it goes beyond the depth limits?* Tyler asked himself. *They always bullshit about the safe depths of these things.* He would be safe, he had to be safe. Dying like this was not an option. In spite of his desperate confidence, Tyler felt a growing terror. Panic would do nothing. He just had to ride it out. Focusing his attention on the controls, he used the suit's inbuilt propulsion and tried to turn himself up the right way.

The growing weight of the cables that had tangled around the armored suit made it difficult to get any traction on the water.

An alarm beeped a depth warning, and a moment later, the suit's lights flickered and went out. Plummeting in pitch darkness, Tyler gave into the flaring sense of panic and screamed.

A few seconds later, lights appeared from below. A steady glow flickering through the flashes from above and the dark shapes already clouding the water around him. *The habitat!* Tyler barely had time to register what he was seeing before the grey ocean floor rushed up and hit him like a concrete wall.

*

Charlie struggled against the forces that dragged him down into the cold mud. He wanted to go up, rise and feel the warmth of the sun on his face again. Not stay down here in the cold, dead darkness. Thrashing his arms to tear free, he opened his eyes. Nari's face stared at him, her own eyes wide in fright, her skin toned yellow by the floating silt and scattered light of her helmet dive lamp.

*"Can you hear me?"* she said, her voice crackling in his ear.

"Yeah," Charlie replied.

*"We need to get into the habitat. It is not safe out here."*

Charlie curled his legs and regained his footing. Standing, he felt more in control, even though the vis was down to only a few feet.

"Where's Billy?" he asked.

*"He's inside."*

"Steve?"

Nari shook her head. *"The habitat is at the end of this line. I've been looking for you for a while now."* She held up a cord wrapped securely around her hand.

"Let's go," he said.

Nari held his hand and took up the slack of the cord as they headed down its length.

The seabed around them was a battlefield of torn metal. Some parts were recognizable; others were broken pieces of larger equipment. "What happened?" Charlie asked.

*"We think there was an explosion on the ship. It sank, a few hundred meters that way."*

Charlie missed where Nari was indicating. "Anyone else injured?"

*"Yes,"* Nari said simply.

They made their way across the broken ground in silence, stepping as lightly as lunar explorers over the debris field.

The habitat had taken a direct hit. The upper sphere lay crushed by a chunk of ship steel that had torn through it before rolling away into the darkness.

Nari led Charlie under the ring of spheres. She climbed a short ladder and vanished through a shimmering surface in a round hatchway. Charlie climbed after her and they emerged out of the water into a cold, circular chamber.

Hooks around the walls held suits of gear. Air tanks stood in metal cages, and Charlie sighed in relief as he took the respirator out of his mouth and inhaled a deep breath of the cold air that smelled metallic but breathable.

"Where's everyone else?" he asked.

"Aroha, Arthur, and Billy are in the central chamber," Nari replied, her voice muffled by the tight neoprene hood she was pulling over her head.

"And everyone else?" Charlie asked again.

Nari's head popped into view, her dark eyes staring up at him with a burning intensity.

"There is no one else," she said.

"Oh… shit…" Charlie felt nausea roll through him. "Casey and Tyler?" he croaked.

"They didn't make it."

Nari unbuckled her BCD and Charlie took the weight of the tanks. Setting them aside before slipping out of his own gear, Nari pulled on a pair of slip-on sneakers, track pants, and a hooded top.

"Have you been in something like this before?" Nari asked.

"Yeah," Charlie admitted. "It's a dive habitat, designed for oil-rigs, prospectors, and scientific use. It provides a shelter, water, air, and supplies for up to ten people. The structure's rated to a depth of a thousand meters. So we're in no danger of the hull collapsing, as long as the internal pressure is maintained. Just one of those things I heard sometime in the last twenty years of being a marine engineer."

Nari scowled at his sarcasm. "Through here." She slid the

handle on a metal door into the OPEN position and pulled the hatch. It swung towards them and Charlie followed Nari through into the central pod.

With the door closed behind them, the air felt warmer and Charlie could hear Aroha speaking in an earnest tone.

The central pod was a cylinder, 30 feet high and 20 feet across. The ceiling divided the cylinder into a snug chamber with a ten-foot ceiling. In the sections above were the utility systems of pipes and communication. The tanks in the base below stored fresh water. Insulation packed into the walls provided protection against the cold water and the same Trimix of gases the divers used in their tanks flowed from a mesh grille in the ceiling.

Bunk beds lined one section of the walls. The rest of the space included a galley and dining area, all lit by halogen lamps bolted to the wall panels.

Aroha sat in a small alcove packed with radio equipment. She had a headset on and was speaking into a microphone, "Mayday, mayday. Can anyone hear me?" she paused and listened to the hum of static coming back.

Arthur sat cross-legged on another bunk; he glanced up when they entered, then went back to polishing his glasses.

"Where's Billy?" Charlie asked.

Nari pointed to where the Samoan lay. Billy was unconscious, his face drained to the grey color of the seabed silt and his right leg bound in splints and bandages.

"What happened?" Charlie asked, moving closer to Billy.

"Falling debris hit him, crushed his leg and cracked his helmet. We were lucky it toppled over so we could get him out.

He's in a bad way," Nari explained.

"We have to get someone down here. We have to get him on a chopper back to the mainland," Charlie insisted.

"Aroha is trying to raise anyone now," Nari said.

"Shit," Aroha said from across the small chamber. "We have no radio. I think the aerial went down with the ship."

"So? Someone's going to notice the floating wreckage. This is one of the busiest fishing spots in the world—"

"The Chatham rise is a rich fishery," Arthur interrupted. "However, the prospecting zone is not part of that. The only hope we have of someone seeing any floating wreckage is if they steam right over the top of it."

"The Air Force. They're always flying around, looking for unauthorized fishing vessels in New Zealand waters."

"It's still not something we can count on," Nari said.

"Fuck!" the Helium in the air made Charlie's voice crack to a high-pitched squeak.

"That's one way of putting it," Arthur murmured.

"We stay calm. We keep safe and we wait," Aroha said.

Charlie took a deep breath and then started talking. "Ascending from this depth will take a long time. Then we will need decompression on the surface. Staying down here, we risk nitrogen narcosis. The air systems here won't run forever. Food and water will run out after a week or two as well. By the time a search starts, there may not be any wreckage to find. We're only a small ship, not a fucking airliner filled with hundreds of passengers. They're not going to spend a lot of time looking for us."

"The top sphere, that's designed for emergency surfacing, right?" Nari asked.

Charlie nodded. "Yeah, but it took one helluva hit from the shit coming down. From the outside, it looked crushed. The interior may still be watertight. Has anyone checked to see what state it's in?"

The two women shook their heads. "We haven't been here long enough to go that far," Aroha said.

"We should conserve our energy," Arthur suggested. "No point in burning through the air we have faster than we need."

Stepping around the two women, Charlie climbed the narrow chrome ladder that led to a round hatch recessed in the ceiling. Twisting the wheel with one hand, he grunted as he pushed against it. The unlocked access door seemed strangely resistant. Bracing himself, Charlie heaved upwards with his entire body weight behind the motion. The seal on the door gave way and a freezing flood of salt water sprayed through the gap.

"Shut the hatch!" Aroha yelled. Charlie choked and spat, blinded by the gushing flow from above. He slipped off the ladder and hung there, his weight pulling the metal door closed. Flexing his arms, he executed a pull-up and grabbed the ladder again with one hand. With the other, he spun the locking wheel shut.

"You bloody idiot!" Arthur's Zen-like calm finally shattered. "If you depressurize the interior, the whole bloody habitat could collapse!"

"I think the top sphere is buggered," Charlie replied.

"No shit?" Aroha snapped.

"Well, that's it. We are F-U-K'ed," Nari said.

For once, Aroha didn't laugh at her friend's way of spelling out swear words.

Arthur slid off the bunk, his feet splashing into the water on the floor as he stood up. "Sit down, all of you. We must remain calm and not give in to panic."

"There must be another way?" Nari asked. "An emergency system?"

"The top sphere *is* the emergency system," Charlie reminded her. She slumped down on a narrow couch that circled the chamber. Arms wrapped around herself, the Indian woman shivered and stared at the floor.

"Doctor Prasad has the right idea." Arthur nodded his approval.

"Maybe we can repair it," Charlie said, returning to floor level. "I'll suit up, go and check on it. It might just need a patch weld or something."

"Great idea," Aroha said, her voice oddly bright. "Say, did you happen to bring an underwater welding torch with you?"

Charlie's mouth opened and then closed again. "I'm just trying to help."

"Well, think more." Aroha turned away and checked a tiny glass porthole in the hatch that led to the next spherical chamber. "I'm going to check the rest of the habitat."

"I'm not sure that's safe," Charlie said.

"Doctor Halligan, I must insist—" Arthur's tone was starting to set Aroha's teeth on edge.

"I can see it's not flooded." Aroha cranked the handle on a

small dynamo torch until it generated enough glow to cast light up the walls.

Armed with the light, she opened the hatch and slipped through, pushing it shut behind her, ignoring the protests of those she left behind.

*

Tyler blinked and shivered against the freezing cold that soaked into his bones. In the pitch darkness, he could feel hard-packed mud under his metal gloves. He groaned and moved his limbs one at a time. Everything seemed to be in working order. "Anyone hear me? Casey...?"

Silence except for the hiss of high-pressure water leaking into his suit. Tyler could taste salt. The leak wasn't dangerous yet; the suit would have filled up drowned him in seconds if it was seriously breached.

Organizing his limbs, Tyler crawled, shaking the mud off and trying to get some idea of where he was. The glow of the habitat lights were about thirty feet away. He leaned on a piece of dull metal and pulled himself into a standing position. The suit sloshed with the water building up inside it; he could feel the freezing chill rising past his knees.

A stream of bubbles rose from the articulated waist section. With probing fingers, Tyler found the hole and pressed his gloves against it, holding the water at bay for now.

"One small step for man... one fucking amazing step for Tyler..."

He looked around, his feet twisting in the cold, dark silt of the ocean floor. Nothing moved out here, and his torchlight caught the gleam of torn steel and other debris that had come down on them when the ship sank.

The damaged habitat reminded Tyler of one of those videos on YouTube, the ones where someone tripped and face-planted into a wedding cake. After the explosion, several tons of steel came down like an axe and split the top sphere before crushing it. That part of the habitat was as much scrap as the ship now spread out over the ground out there in the darkness.

Bubbles were streaming out from under the walkway that ringed the habitat. Somewhere in there, one of the spheres was leaking air. As the pressure changed, water would flow in. Anyone inside would drown if the leak wasn't fixed.

A current swirled past him, giving shape to a darker shadow in the periphery of his vision. Tyler breathed and stared, eyes scanning in time with the sweep of his helmet mounted lights.

A shark came gliding out of the darkness, indifferent to the tiny human standing on the barren seafloor. Tyler watched it, breathing slowly, letting the fish move on and ignore him, just like it was doing right now.

The second shark struck a glancing blow on the shoulder of his suit, biting into a floating mat of foam insulation inches from Tyler's head.

"Fuck!" the diver yelped, flailing as he tried to maintain his balance.

More sharks emerged from the darkness. Tyler thought they might be great whites. Casey's bullshit advice about identifying them from their tails had gone completely as his mind blanked in terror.

In the span of three rasping breaths, Tyler counted six sharks. All at least ten feet long and moving in an eerily synchronized pattern. *They can't be great whites*, Tyler reasoned. *Great white's only come together to breed. They hang out on their own. They don't hunt in packs. Not like this. Right?*

Two of the sharks changed direction, each approaching a pale lump sinking down through the dark water. Tyler stared, trying to make sense of what he was seeing. It was a person's leg, torn off above the knee and the ankle waving at a strange angle. The two predators coordinated their strike, each turning at the last moment to engulf half the meat. Tyler felt his nausea rising.

In seconds, only a few drifting scraps remained of the leg, and they were quickly devoured by the scavenging fish who huddled close to the shark's larger bodies.

Walking with all the care and concentration of a very drunk person, Tyler made his way towards the habitat.

A shark emerged from the darkness, shooting towards Tyler like a torpedo. He twisted, stumbling in the heavy steel suit and shuffling into the shadow under the habitat. He felt the shark bump against him before it turned away in search of easier prey.

*More than one*, Tyler reminded himself. *There's more than one out here. Get the fuck inside right now.*

Twisting to look in every direction at once clouded Tyler's view in a swirl of bubbles and floating particulates. He thought sharks hunted by smell. He wasn't bleeding, but there was lots of blood in the water. Enough to bring every killer fish from here to Australia.

Tyler walked under the habitat, aware of the sharks patrolling around him as they circled in the endless hunt for meat.

He kept moving, reaching the ladder. The rippling circle that marked the divers' entrance waiting overhead. He looked around one more time, checking for any inquisitive predators.

The water in the suit had risen to his waist and he could barely breathe in the freezing cold. Without someone to work the winch and chains to lift the suit out of the water, he was stuck down here.

"Oh for fuck's sake," Tyler muttered and banged on the ladder with an armored fist.

*

"Fiberglass patches," Charlie announced. He had spent the last five minutes searching the supplies they had on board for anything that could help him repair the damaged habitat shell. "I can cut them to fit, apply underwater epoxy adhesive and she'll be as good as new."

Billy hadn't moved or spoken since he got in here, Nari's stare remained fixed on the floor, and Arthur seemed to be sulking because no one listened to him.

Charlie's enthusiasm flagged. "I'm going to check the outside."

Returning to the open divers' entrance, Charlie slithered into his drysuit again. The air was close to freezing, and he felt goosebumps rising on his arms as he zipped up the neoprene and rubber suit. The dive computer showed he had enough air for a fifteen-minute excursion into the dark. Plenty of time to go around the habitat and assess the damage done.

The dive ladder vibrated with the dull clang of ringing metal.

Turning to the circular hole in the floor, Charlie frowned at the white shape blurred through the water. A metal hand broke the surface and waved.

Charlie reached out and grabbed it. Even in the water, the weight of the dive suit was impossible to lift on his own. Letting go, he did a quick search of the dive chamber until he found what he needed.

Breathing slowly through his respirator, Charlie sank into the dark water and felt around the dive suit. He could see the young diver from the ship, *Tyler?* talking loudly, but the sound was blocked by the thick glass faceplate of his helmet.

Charlie waved the end of the thick cable he held, and then worked his way around the suit, finding a socket with a torn cable hanging from it like a severed umbilical cord.

Twisting the dead line out of the socket, he replaced it with the comms cable from the habitat.

*"-king drowning!"* Tyler shouted.

"This is Charlie, can you hear me?"

*"Charlie? Get me the fuck out of this thing!"*

"Hang on. We don't have anything strong enough to lift you out. You're going to need to exit the suit. I'll help you. Then we can get you inside."

*"I'll fucking die!"*

Charlie moved to where Tyler could see him. "You won't die. The suit is leaking; if it had lost pressure all at once, it would have killed you already. Now you might have a chance. You just need to trust me."

Tyler looked pale and scared, so Charlie gave him an OK

sign.

"Get ready." Charlie ran his hands over the suit, looking for the locks on the seals. He flicked the latches and held on as the remaining gasses inside the suit bubbled outwards.

Heaving the suit open, he grabbed the struggling Tyler and shoved him upwards into the cold air of the habitat.

Tyler rolled across the metal floor, coughing and shivering. Beside him, Charlie surfaced, pulling his dive mask off and hanging on to the edge of the portal.

"I think I know a way we can get out of here, all of us. Safely," Charlie said.

"Get out! Sharks are fu-fu-fucking every-where," Tyler replied through chattering teeth. He moved on to his knees, reaching for a towel hanging from a nearby hook.

"Get inside and get—" Charlie's voice cut off with a splash.

"Mate?" Tyler stood up and turned around, shivering so hard he could barely move.

The water in the dive portal boiled pink. A dark shape rolled and Charlie's hand rose and fell, the gloved fingers twitching. Tyler stared in frozen shock. Something hit Charlie's body from below and dragged it out of sight.

"Fuck me…" Tyler whimpered.

*

Aroha knew about sharks, she liked all aspects of diving, and being under the water was always preferable to being on it; boats weren't her thing at all. The cramped space of the habitat felt like the bowels of a ship and the tight space made her feel claustrophobic.

The spheres around the central cylinder housed the systems to filter air, batteries to power the electronics, sealed containers of food and fresh water. The toilet was in a cubicle the size of an old phone box and looked like it belonged in an airplane. She used it and flushed into the open water.

Checking the next sphere, she hesitated and peered through the tiny glass porthole. It was dark in there and Aroha felt confident that if her memory of the layout was correct, the heavy-duty batteries that provided the habitat with lights and heat were in that steel room.

Straining, Aroha pulled on the lever that opened the door. It creaked and then water started to gush around her feet. Pushing back, Aroha closed the door again. The room was filling with water. The batteries were sealed and waterproof, but she didn't know if the rest of the wiring would be.

Turning around, she made her way back through the outer ring of spherical chambers to the dive sphere, which she thought of as being like a veranda.

Aroha opened the door and found Tyler staring at the calm water. "Tyler?"

He looked at her and nodded, his skin grey with cold.

"Oh my God, are you okay? Come on, let's get you inside and warmed up." She helped Tyler to his feet and guided him into the central chamber.

Wrapping him in a blanket and rubbing his head with a dry towel, she called for Nari to come and help. Nari climbed off her bunk and padded over. "He's risking hypothermia. We need to warm him up."

Arthur watched silently as Nari and Aroha moved Tyler to the bunk. Aroha climbed on first, then Tyler lay down next to her. Nari covered them both with blankets.

Tyler tried to tell them about Charlie but only managed to stammer his name.

"Billy?" he asked as he managed to catch his breath.

"He's got a concussion and is unconscious. He should be okay though," Nari replied.

The shivering eased as Tyler's body temperature began to rise. He felt desperately tired, but the image of Charlie's hand reaching for him flared in his mind every time he closed his eyes.

"Charlie was going to check outside, did you see him?" Aroha asked from her position spooned against Tyler.

"He... he was in the water," Tyler said. "I think a shark attacked him."

"What?" Aroha sat up, almost banging her head against the top bunk. "A shark? Seriously?"

Tyler nodded. "I think so. I didn't see it. But there's sharks all over the place out there. They're feeding on scraps and stuff from the explosion."

"Stuff?" Aroha asked.

"Yeah..." Tyler didn't elaborate. "Charlie said that he knew how to get us back to the surface."

"How?" Nari and Aroha both leaned forward, faces bright with hope.

"He didn't have a chance to explain. He just said there was a way. I've been trying to work it out. The top-sphere, it's fucked, I mean it's messed up."

"Yeah, Charlie tried that already and it's flooded up there," Aroha replied.

"I saw bubbles, there's air leaking out of the habitat. I can patch any leaks. There's cold weld patches. Fabric stuff, like a bulletproof vest. We can glue it over holes, fill cracks with epoxy, and try pumping the water out."

"That was what Charlie was talking about. He had that stuff with him when he left." Nari shivered.

"How did you get down here?" Arthur's voice cut in.

"I dunno," Tyler answered. He tried to shrug, but was wracked with shivering instead.

"You were in the hardsuit? Did it survive?" Arthur climbed off his bunk and crossed the room. "Where is the hardsuit?"

"I- It's outside. It was filling up with water. Charlie got me out and I guess we left it there."

Arthur turned and headed out to the dive chamber without further comment.

"Get warm," Aroha said. "We'll get you some food, and once you've warmed up, we can work out what to do."

*

Arthur shivered in the chill air of the open dive chamber. The water under the portal was lit by lights in the base of the habitat, and he could see the blurred shape of the armored dive suit lying on its side a tantalizing ten feet away.

Taking one of the dry suits from the rack, he dressed, double-checking everything as he went. With the weight belt, BCD, and helmet on and secured, he took a careful breath. The mix of oxygen, helium and nitrogen shouldn't taste like anything, yet

Arthur always thought there was a metallic tang to the air.

On the far wall of the dive chamber, a gantry for a steel rope cable and winch was locked against the wall with a slide-bolt. He freed it and swung the pivot arm out. A chain hung down with a cross bar, and two chains off each end. At the end of those chains were large aluminum hooks, perfect for lifting a heavy object, like a metal dive suit, up into the habitat.

Arthur pushed the green button on the control switch; the electric engine whirred and the chains vanished into the water. With a testicle-shrinking sense of unease, Arthur climbed down the ladder, through the surface of the water, and into the cold below.

At the bottom of the ladder, he crouched down, looking in all directions at once, trying to see if any shark was bearing down on him. The water was clear for now, only shadows were dancing to the twitching beam of his halogen lights.

Satisfied he was safe for now, Arthur took the hooks on the end of their chains and fastened them to the receiving rings on the back of the dive suit's shoulders.

His nerve failing, he scuttled back up the ladder. Struggling out onto the deck, he lay there and pulled his helmet off. Arthur panted in irrational terror. *You can do this.*

After a minute, he stood up and activated the winch. The engine's pitch dropped as it took the strain of the load. Slowly, the steel suit rose from the bottom like a marionette. Arthur watched intently as the discarded suit rose into the habitat. Seawater gushed out of the suit, pouring into the portal and turning the surface to foam.

With the suit in position on the deck, Arthur checked the internal systems. The electronics were secure under waterproof layers for safe operation in any circumstances. While the suit was designed for umbilical air-supply, it could be fitted with Trimix tanks and a respirator valve connector at the back of the helmet.

The boy had said the suit was leaking. Arthur ran his fingers over the dense rubber and plastic of the articulated joints. A pin-sized hole could be deadly at this depth. The crushing pressure of the water would force its way in and flood the suit.

Arthur hesitated, and scraped at a spot on the back of the suit's knee joint. Under his cold fingers, he could feel a small cut in the rubber, less than an inch long; it could be where the water was coming from.

Charlie had left the bag of patching supplies and epoxy glue on the deck of the dive chamber. Arthur applied a thick smear of the foul-smelling gunk to the paler side of the industrial fabric. Starting at the side, Arthur wrapped the grey strip around the knee of the steel suit like a bandage. Keeping it tight and smoothing it down with one hand, he got a good seal. The knee joint wouldn't bend without risking tearing the seal, but what Arthur had in mind didn't require any knee flexing.

\*

"I'll go," Tyler heard his own voice saying the words and couldn't quite believe it.

"We don't even know if it would work," Aroha said.

"I'll go," Tyler said with more conviction. "I'll go outside. I'll check the damage and make any repairs that I can.

"Be careful," Aroha said. "The sharks will be snapping up any easy food. You can scare them off by hitting the nose. Try not to thrash around. Move slowly and keep an eye on your surroundings."

Tyler nodded. The residue of salt in his throat still burned and made it hard to speak.

"I'll give you a hand to suit up," Aroha said and gave Tyler a smile that made him realize he would swim to the surface for this woman if she asked him to.

Aroha cranked the steel door to the dive chamber open. Tyler pulled on it and the greased hinges worked silently.

"Hey!" he yelled. Aroha followed him into the cold room, and the white helmet of the hardsuit was vanishing in a storm of bubbles through the floor.

"Arthur?" Aroha stared at the rolling water in stunned surprise.

"He's fucking nuts!" Tyler yelled. Racing to the controls, he hit the red button and stopped the winch. Under the surface, the wavering shape of the hardsuit thrashed, twisting the winch chains.

"Bring him back!" Aroha yelled.

Tyler flicked a switch on the winch control. The direction of the motor now reversed, he pressed the green button and the winch whined as it took the weight of the load.

The pitch rose and the chains locked tight.

"Is he stuck?" Tyler asked, peering over the edge of the portal.

"I think he's hanging on to one of the base struts?" Aroha

couldn't be sure.

"Where does he think he is going to go?"

"He must be trying for the surface." Tyler's thumb was pressed white against the control button, as if applying extra pressure might somehow add to the electric winch's power.

The cables whined with tension and then whipped through the water as they went slack.

"Did the cables snap?" Aroha crouched at the water's edge as the wire lines were wound in.

"Nah, I think he unhooked them."

"Sonnovabitch," Aroha muttered. Standing up, she turned on the spot, unable to pace in the small chamber. "Okay, so he starts to surface. What happens to him? Can he reach the surface safely?"

Tyler secured the wire cables out of the way and hung the control box on its hook. "Well, yeah I guess. But, he's been down here for a while so he'll need to decompress. That could take a few days. He'll suffocate before then. The drysuit usually works on umbilical air-supply. If he's got Trimix tanks on it, then he's got a few hours max."

"That idiot." Aroha glared at the water.

"His only chance is if a rescue ship is nearby or he can let off some flares or something to attract attention. Then they need to get him into a decompression chamber, or keep him supplied with air and slowly reduce the pressure in the suit."

"Hang on, weren't you going to go straight back up?" Aroha folded her arms and regarded Tyler critically.

"Yeah, but I wasn't going anywhere near this deep. Also, the atmosphere I was in was pressurized to the surface, so no danger there. And yeah, I wasn't going to be down long enough to risk the bends."

"Fuck," Aroha said.

"Yeah." Tyler nodded, embarrassed to hear the blonde woman cursing.

"I should go out, see what the damage is." Tyler went to the rack of drysuits and started working his way into one while Aroha stood by awkwardly unsure of how she could help.

"Can you zip me up?" Tyler turned and waved at the zipper that ran up his back. Aroha put one hand on his shoulder and pulled it up, then pressed the sealing Velcro flaps over it.

"Cheers," Tyler said. A weird tingling on his back where he sensed Aroha's touch.

"BCD?" Aroha asked.

"Weight belt first." Tyler took the heavy belt with its lead ballast from a hook and clipped it around his waist. "Okay, now the BCD."

The scientist lifted the Trimix set, her arms flexing as she held the frame ready for Tyler to slip the straps over his shoulders. A moment later, he straightened up and clipped everything together.

"All good?" she asked.

"Yeah." Tyler felt weird at the attention. He liked girls. He liked them a lot. Aroha was not like the girls he had dated or hooked up with. She was hot and really smart. Older too, but not old like his mom. It made her confusing.

"Helmet, fins," Aroha said, handing them to him. Tyler got

everything in place and flashed an OK gesture at Aroha.

"Hey," she said as he sat down on the edge of the water. Tyler twisted and looked up.

"Be careful."

Tyler nodded, blushing a little under his mask. He took a breath from his respirator and slipped into the water.

Moving easily, Tyler came out from under the clover-shaped group of spheres. He found the service ladder that curved up the outside and clambered up, the beams from his halogen lights swinging as he looked in all directions at once. A walkway circled the base of the top sphere and he could see a tangle of fallen steel that had slammed into it. Reaching carefully, he pulled himself over the first obstacle: thick steel that had twisted like toffee under the force of the explosion.

He couldn't see the white shell of the hard suit anywhere. Arthur was probably out of visual range by now and rising steadily.

Ahead of Tyler, bubbles streamed out through the wreckage. Somewhere under the tangled mess, a crack in the top sphere was letting air escape. As the pressure changed, water would flow in. If the door between the spheres didn't hold, the survivors inside would drown in a freezing deluge.

Climbing up the curve of the habitat sphere, Tyler glanced at his dive computer; he still had time before he was in real danger of running out of air. A primal panic teased at the fringes of his mind. He wanted to run, or swim, for the surface. Find a boat and get the hell out of the water.

A pale shape emerged from the darkness, the shark's

cartilaginous body flexing as it swam slowly past, the dead black eyes chilling Tyler more than the water pressing in on all sides.

*Remember why you are out here. Stay focused on the job.* Tyler tested the weight of the metal debris. Setting his feet, he sank into a squat and heaved upwards. With a dull shriek, a slab of metal twisted away from the broken sphere. Tyler pushed it far enough for gravity to take over and the metal tumbled to the ground, landing with a thud that sent a cloud of silt rising a few feet into the water.

More than anything, Tyler wanted to be useful, to take something back that would impress Aroha. Finding the source of the leak and fixing it would save everyone.

He took another look around and then went back to clearing the wreckage.

# CHAPTER 7

*Chatham Rise South Pacific Ocean, Longitude 44° S, Latitude 176° W. 400 meters below the surface.*

Just how he survived the plummeting descent to the bottom was a mystery to Casey. The tumbling chaos of the ship's interior had sent him crashing along a flooded corridor. He managed to pull himself into a cabin and seal the door against a roaring tempest of escaping air and inrushing water. Now at the bottom, the pressure in the room was equalizing as it flooded.

Taking a deep breath of the chemical mix of air in his tanks, Casey set his feet and heaved on the twisted slab of metal door. The bottom of the ocean was not like the moon, where everything weighed a lot less. Down here, it was all about water displacement. The volume of things displaced water and the water pushed things up depending on their volume. It was why an airbag could raise a pallet of gold from a sunken wreck. The air pumped into the bag increased its volume and created positive buoyancy.

The increased buoyancy was as close to being on the moon as

Casey would ever get and didn't mean shit when he was trying to lift metal that weighed as much as he did.

He swallowed his nausea from the roller coaster ride of his descent. The interior of the ship had turned upside down and anything not bolted down had become a torpedo, more than capable of crushing or impaling him.

When the door toppled over, Casey had already moved out of the way. Silt and floating debris obscured his view. It would settle in time. Anything edible would be eaten, and the rest would sink the last few feet to the bottom or float away on the endless currents. Algae and deep-sea fish would colonize the wreckage. Until then, anything left was available for Casey to take and use to survive.

Cracking a chemlight, he twisted through the doorway and brushed the worst of the floating crap aside. The demolition charges had torn through the hull below the water line and allowed the force of the sea to sweep the softer interior with more force than the explosion of fire. He found himself in one of the narrow corridors that ran between the top deck and the bowels of the ship where the engine room and other drive systems took up all the available space.

Casey moved down the corridor, the water lit with a luminescent green glow from the light stick he had clipped to his BCD. He stopped when he came to a deck plan on the wall. He was on the starboard interior deck. The ship had come down on its left or port side, which made navigation even more confusing. He checked his dive computer, confirming he had plenty of time to find what he needed and get out.

Tracing a gloved finger along the diagram, he tapped on his target. The room he needed to get to was four doors along from his current position. Pushing off, Casey swam down the corridor he had walked along only that morning. The door opened inwards, and because it was on the downward side of the ship, it fell away as soon as he twisted the handle. The air trapped inside exploded upwards in a cloud of bubbles that hit with enough force to send the diver careening into the opposite wall.

After recovering his breath and orientation, Casey swam down pulling himself into the radio room and looked around.

The damage to the communication's equipment was terminal. Bullet holes had made shiny divots in the metal casings of the radios, allowing saltwater to destroy the delicate electronics inside.

Porno magazines, floating like stingrays, and a couple of empty gear bags sunken against the opposite wall were the only obvious items left behind.

Digging through the trash, Casey searched the room for any handheld waterproof radios. The cabinet where they were kept had remained shut during the sinking. Casey pried the catch open and the small cupboard belched a bubble of air.

A heartbeat later, Casey propelled himself backwards to collide against the opposite wall. The cabinet was empty, except for the red light of an explosive charge blinking in the cold water.

Casey's breath exploded through his respirator, his rapid breathing exceeding the volume of the system and leaving him short of breath. He couldn't see if the counter was going down, or if opening the door had somehow activated the explosive. He twisted and swam to the door. A foam mattress drifting in from the corridor blocked his way, and Casey scrambled to push the squishy block aside as unfamiliar panic threatened to choke him.

Crawling out through the doorway, Casey felt his skin crawl with rising terror. If the charges were powerful enough to tear holes through the steel hull, the detonation could easily kill him.

With a steady beat of his fins, Casey swam blindly down the corridor towards the door. The amount of crap floating in the water had reduced visibility to near zero. He swam right into the steel frame and recoiled, half-stunned. The door had twisted when the ship went down and was now jammed open with a gap of only a few inches.

Casey curled his fingers around the door and heaved on it. *Fuck.* In a few seconds, the interior of the ship would disintegrate and Casey would be another red smear of fish food.

Twisting around, Casey swept the flashlight over the ceiling. The air vents were no bigger than playing cards. Years of watching James Bond movies didn't offer any solutions.

A metallic thud vibrated through the water, the unnatural sound taking Casey by surprise. He pushed away from the wall and put his hand out, feeling the metal in case it happened again.

The second blow was more insistent and was followed by the deep bass moan of stiff metal creaking as warped hinges turned.

Casey angled his flashlight at the widening gap in the closed hatch. A length of steel slid into view and the person on the other side levered the jammed door open. Casey didn't bother waiting for an invitation. He pushed up through the open hatch and collided with the other diver. In her brief expression of surprise, he saw the face of First Mate, Kelly. She swam upwards, trailing in Casey's wake as he swam away from the wreck and up into the dark water.

The charge detonated a second later, the shockwave ripping through the water, sending both divers tumbling in a chaotic vortex of swirling debris.

Casey breathed; the adrenaline of being so close to death again was exhausting. He felt a deep chill in his bones as he wished for nothing more than a hot cup of coffee and a soft bed.

Kelly was floating limp in the water, her body just another piece of torn wreckage drifting in the darkness. Casey swam towards the glowing beacon of her helmet light. A pair of sharks emerged from the darkness, swimming with the casual swagger of apex predators as they homed in on the unconscious woman. Casey yelled into his respirator, waving his arms and trying to distract the killer fish. He couldn't see if Kelly was bleeding, but nothing else would have the two great whites homing in on her like a pair of guided torpedoes.

The first shark turned, its jaws opening wide as it crashed into Kelly at waist height. The grey shape convulsed, twisting and tearing as it bit down, through the neoprene drysuit, through flesh and bone. The second shark's mouth opened like a bear trap and sprang closed on Kelly's shoulder, separating limb from torso in one great, tearing bite.

Casey felt his gorge rising. Throwing up down here would be bad; he'd probably choke on it. Kelly's remains vanished in a cloud of blood, rendered grey by the lack of light. The sharks made short work of the scraps, and within a minute, the woman's body was gone.

# CHAPTER 8

*Chatham Rise South Pacific Ocean, Longitude 44° S, Latitude 176° W. 400 meters below the surface.*

"Why don't we just surface and let off a flare or something?" Nari asked.

Aroha replied immediately, "Because we are between the mainland and the Chatham Islands. We can't guarantee that a ship will be anywhere nearby, and we have as much chance of drowning on the surface as we do down here."

"Arthur thought it was worth a try."

"Arthur is an idiot. He's abandoned the rest of us in a stupid attempt to save his own ass!" Aroha was still fuming about the geologist escaping on his own.

"At least he's doing something! If we stay here, we will die. If we surface, at least we have a chance!"

Aroha didn't know how to respond. Instead, she put her hand on Billy's forehead. The Samoan had been unconscious for an hour now and she wondered if he might ever wake up. "We can't move Billy. At least not until he wakes up and we can assess him properly."

Nari paused in her pacing of the small chamber. "Do you think we are cursed?"

"I don't know about you, but I'm definitely cursed."

"Your brother," Nari said immediately. "I am sorry, I did not mean to make you think of him."

"I was supposed to be back in time for Dave's funeral," Aroha said. "God help my parents if they have to hold memorial services for both of us."

"I wish Tyler would hurry up," Nari said, changing the subject.

"We shouldn't have let him go outside." Aroha sounded distracted, lost in the memories of her brother's recent death.

The locking wheel on the steel door that led to the dive room spun. Both women turned to watch; it couldn't be anyone but Tyler, though they still had some hope.

The young diver blinked when he realized that Aroha and Nari were staring at him.

"Are you okay?" Nari asked.

"Uh, yeah. I mean, shit," Tyler said.

"Did you find the source of the leak?" Aroha asked.

Tyler nodded. "Top sphere, it's fucked. Crushed, by a big chunk of wreckage."

"*Mardachod!*" Nari cursed.

Aroha frowned in concentration. "Okay, that confirms why our communications array is out. We could float a cable to the surface. Broadcast a signal up the wire and hope that someone picks up the message."

"Yeah, that would work. We could inflate a dive bag and tie the cable to it," Tyler nodded.

"The communications cable, that connected us to the ship, we could try floating that?" Aroha looked hopeful.

"I think it's still outside. If not, there will be a lot of it somewhere on the ship," Tyler added.

"When can we go and get it?" Nari asked.

Tyler chewed his lip, his desire to be the hero challenged by his nervousness. "I'd like to eat and warm up first. We should give everything a chance to settle. There's a shit-load of silt and floating crap in the water at the moment." He hoped that once the sharks had eaten their fill, they would also move on in search of fresh prey.

"Of course, you're right." Aroha grabbed a blanket and flapped it until the micro-fleece unfolded. "Wrap up, I'll find some food."

Their first meal consisted of noodles heated on a small electric element. Aroha stirred in a tube of fish paste protein and served enough for the three of them.

"How long with the lights last?" Nari asked, cradling a hot bowl of noodles in her hands.

"I don't know," Aroha replied. "There's batteries that were charged by the currents driving a generator fan on the top sphere. If that's all gone, maybe a few more hours?"

"Without electricity, what happens to the habitat?" Nari asked.

Tyler spoke up, keen to show the two women he could help.

"There's back up Trimix tanks. They're still secure. The filters that scrub the CO2 out of the air, they don't need electricity. See they have—"

"I have a Master's degree in chemistry and a Doctorate in sedimentary bio-chemistry," Nari snapped. "I know how a carbon-dioxide scrubber works!"

Tyler subsided into a sulking scowl, glaring at his bowl of noodles.

"Maybe we should all try and get some sleep?" Aroha said into the cold silence. "We can't do anything right now, and I'm sure we'll feel better with clear heads."

Nari put her untouched food down and walked off to lay down on one of the narrow bunks. Wrapping up in a blanket, she rolled over and faced the wall.

Aroha and Tyler ate in silence, the steam from the cooling noodles adding to the pervading damp.

"Which bunk do you want?" Aroha asked, putting her empty plate aside.

"I dunno, whichever, I guess."

Aroha went and made a nest for herself in an empty bunk. Tyler scraped the last of the noodles out of his bowl and wondered if he should use the bathroom before going to sleep. A moment later, he cocked his head, listening to a scraping sound that came from the underside of the habitat. The currents weren't strong enough to move the metal wreckage and a fish wouldn't make that much noise. Tyler went to the metal doorway that sealed the dive entrance off from their quarters. Peering through the tiny glass porthole, he tried to see into the gloom. A moment later, a pale face appeared on the other side.

"Casey!" Tyler shouted and grabbed the locking wheel. Spinning it open, he heaved the door wide.

Casey stumbled into the sphere, shaking and pale. "Fuck me," he said. "Fuck me."

The two scientists crowded around, everyone asking questions and trying to tell their own version of events all at once.

Casey waved them to silence. "Where's Billy?" he asked.

"He was injured. A broken leg. He passed out when I splinted it," Aroha explained.

"Anyone else?"

The survivors of the dive shook their heads. Casey sat down on a plastic crate.

"I found Kelly, you know? The first mate? She'd managed to get into dive gear and secured herself in the ship when the shooting started."

"Wait, what? Shooting? What the hell happened up there?" Aroha demanded.

Casey took a deep breath and explained what he knew; South African mercenaries, apparently paid to destroy the ship by some extremist environmentalist, had scuttled the vessel.

"That is the most insane thing I have ever heard!" Aroha looked like she wanted to laugh.

Casey continued, "I was on the ship when they started killing everyone. It was the camera guy and his crew. They seemed pretty professional when it came to blowing shit up."

"The captain, did he make a distress call?" Nari asked.

"I don't think so. The radio room got smashed up."

"Where is Kelly now?" Nari asked.

"She… didn't make it," Casey replied.

The others stood in silence, aware that they were facing the same fate.

"We need to get out of here," Nari said. "We were talking about sending the communications cable to the surface and then transmitting a distress signal on a radio frequency."

"The radio transmission gear is in the top sphere," Casey said. "From what I saw, that's pretty much gone."

"Yeah, it's fucked," Tyler agreed.

"How are we going to get help then?" Nari threw her hands up in frustration. "Honestly, this kind of thing must happen to other expeditions. Someone must know we are missing?"

"Not for a week, maybe ten days," Casey said. "If there is an oil slick on the surface, or floating debris, that could raise the alarm."

"How far is it to the Chatham's do y'reckon?" Tyler asked.

Casey shook his head. "At least three hundred k's. We aren't swimming to land."

"I am not going to just sit here and wait to die!" Nari's voice cracked as she yelled, her eyes brimming with tears of panic.

"Nari, it's going to be okay. We will work something out." Casey lowered his voice. "Right now, we just need to take stock and make sure we are safe."

"We're running on batteries for the lights and heat," Aroha said. "The air filters are chemical, so we can keep breathing for a few days. We'll probably die of hypothermia before then."

"Look, I know you're scared. But we will get you both out of here safely," Casey said. "Tyler, get some sleep. Same with the rest of you; we will all operate better after a few hours' kip."

Tyler retreated to an empty bunk without comment.

Nari went back to her bunk and curled up under blankets.

"I should have been a lawyer. That is what my father wanted. Either a lawyer or a doctor like my brother,"

"Nari'll be okay. She's the most intelligent person I have ever met," Aroha said.

"Don't suppose either of you are secretly engineers?" Casey asked.

Aroha flashed a weak grin. "No, sorry. Completely useless."

They stood in silence for a moment, neither making eye contact.

"I-I'm sorry about your brother," Casey managed after the silence grew uncomfortable.

"You said that back in Lyttelton."

"Well yeah, but I was drunk."

"You could have mentioned that you were going on this expedition at the time."

"Really drunk," Casey added.

"I don't normally do that, you know. Fall into bed with some random stranger."

"Why not?"

"Because, well... I just don't."

"One night stands are one thing, it does get awkward when you find yourselves on a research ship the next day, though."

"Christ, does it ever." Aroha looked away again.

"Look, we had a good time. You were okay with it, weren't

you?"

"Of course, I'm not saying you did anything uninvited. I just… it was just weird."

Casey grinned in spite of himself.

"I don't mean like that," Aroha blushed. "I'm going to get some sleep."

Casey found a bottle of water and an energy bar. He ate while the others slept. The image of Kelly's eyes flaring wide with agonized shock appearing in front of him when he closed his eyes.

# CHAPTER 9

*Chatham Rise South Pacific Ocean, Longitude 44° S,
Latitude 176° W. 400 meters below the surface.*

Tyler woke to the sound of water dripping and then blinked as a
cold drop splatted on his face. Rolling off the bunk, he looked
up. A narrow snake-like line of water ran down the curved wall;
it appeared to be coming from a seam in the insulation.

"Ah shit," he muttered.

"Whazzit?" Aroha said from her bunk across the small room.

"Water's coming in from somewhere," Tyler whispered.

Aroha kicked off her blankets and hurried over to peer up at
the ceiling.

"Shit," she agreed.

"I'll suit up, go out, and see if I can find any more cracks. The
patching I did might not be enough."

"Where's Casey?" Aroha looked around the small spherical
room, checking he wasn't lurking in the shadows.

"I dunno, maybe he went out already?"

"What's going on?" Nari peered down at them over the edge

of the second tier bunk.

"Nothing." Aroha gave Tyler a warning glance. He shrugged and headed off to the dive chamber.

"Where's Casey?" Nari asked as she climbed down to the floor.

"He went out for milk," Tyler replied.

"The sphere is leaking?" Nari pulled on extra layers of dry clothing, her breath misting in the air.

"Yes," Aroha agreed. "Tyler is going out to check the damage and see if he can patch it."

"I always thought I would want to be buried at sea. Not like this, though. I wanted to be cremated first, then have my ashes scattered." Nari swept her dark hair out of the collar of her jacket.

"Nobody is going to die."

"We are already dead," Nari replied with a cold certainty.

*

Tyler closed the steel door behind him, but left it unlocked. Casey sat on an upturned storage crate at the edge of the dive entrance. He stared into the water and didn't look up when Tyler approached.

"Hey, boss. You okay?"

"She's right you know." Casey's eyes reflected the light shining off the water. "We are dead. We can't use compressed air and surface without decompression. The return would have been long and slow anyway, even with the dive bell."

Tyler nodded; dying seemed like something that happened to other people. It had an abstract sense to it. Someone would rescue them and then this would just be a great story to tell chicks at the pub.

"Someone'll come and find us, aye?"

Casey looked up, his expression pale and drawn. "No."

"We can rig a big set of tanks, enough to breathe during a decompression dive. Regular stops, should take a few hours to get up there."

Casey shook his head. "You reach the surface, then what? Swim to New Zealand? Or go the other way, Chatham Islands?"

"Let off a flare, there's fishing boats and shit."

"Even if you did get there and it's not blowing a bloody storm, shark's will come and have you before anyone sees your flare."

"Nah, you said that sharks are harmless." Tyler grinned, sensing his boss was joking with him.

"I was wrong," Casey said. "I was really fucking wrong."

A cold fist clenched in Tyler's gut.

Casey's hands were shaking and his eyes were shining. "There's some fucked-up shit going on out there. I keep thinking I have to go out again. Go out and find a way to get a signal to the surface. Keep us all safe and get everyone home. But every time I blink, I see Kelly from the ship. I see her face when the sharks got her."

"Sharks?" Tyler looked at the circular pool that marked the border between the habitat and the ocean. "I thought she was like, injured or drowned or something."

"Nah, mate. Sharks tore her to pieces, right in front of me."

"Charlie, too," Tyler whispered. "Took him right there. You

going to tell the girls?"

Casey sprang to his feet. "Of course I'm not fucking telling them. You keep your fucking mouth shut, too. Understand?"

"Yeah, okay." Tyler backed away in the narrow space. The water next to him rippled and a surge washed over his feet.

A long grey shape swam under the habitat, the smooth and graceful motion of a shark that vanished from view a second later.

"You think they are hunting us maybe?" Tyler's eyes were wide with speculation.

"They're sharks, Tyler. Sharks don't hunt people. That's lions or polar bears or something."

"That was not a fucking polar bear."

"Keep your damned voice down." Casey checked the door into the main chamber. "Suit up, there are more leaks in the spheres and we need to see how bad it is."

"I know." Tyler lifted his chin. "I told Aroha I would see if I could patch it."

Casey nodded. "Good plan. You fix it, I'll watch for man-eating sharks."

"Do we have any more underwater patches?" Tyler asked. "I found one box and underwater epoxy resin seemed to do the job."

Casey looked around the cramped chamber. "There should be more around here somewhere. Of course, if we had a fully equipped and supported surface team, we could weld it."

"Think it will hold?" Tyler shivered as he pulled on the cold neoprene drysuit.

"Doesn't matter. As long as it gives us another day or a few hours. Wait for me here." Casey yanked the door open and went inside the habitat.

"Everything okay?" Aroha asked. Her hands wrapped around a steaming mug of tea.

"Yeah, just gearing up to patch the leak." Casey twisted the locking handle on the secondary hatch that led to the next sphere. As he cracked the seal, the rim of the door immediately sprayed water in a high-pressure fountain, only the remaining latch preventing it from exploding inwards.

"Shit!" Casey set his feet and pressed against the tons of seawater trying to pour through the millimeter gap. His ears popped as the pressure changed. Aroha dropped her cup and ran to help. Together, they leaned on the door until Casey could wind the lock shut.

"I guess the leak is worse than we thought," Casey said, wiping the salt water from his face.

"We should check the other compartments again," Aroha suggested.

"No!" Nari yelled from her position on the high bunk. "If they are all flooded, you will kill us."

"She's got a point," Casey agreed. "I'll go outside and check if there are bubbles or stuff being sucked into the spheres."

Aroha leaned in close. "You need to get us out of here. Billy's injured. Nari's not coping, and I am shit-scared."

Casey nodded. "It'll be okay."

Her expression said she did not believe him, which was fine with Casey; he didn't feel confident either.

# CHAPTER 10

*Chatham Rise South Pacific Ocean, Longitude 44° S, Latitude 176° W. 400 meters below the surface.*

The dark water embraced the two divers in cold pressure. Casey turned slowly, the beams from his helmet lights diffusing in the gloom after less than a hundred feet.

He gave an OK hand gesture to Tyler, who returned it, and then moved out from under the habitat.

Like two astronauts on a spacewalk, they climbed up the side of the spherical shell marked '4'. Debris from the scuttled ship had spread over some distance, and Casey considered them lucky that the entire habitat hadn't been completely crushed.

Tyler set his feet on a ladder and pulled on a chunk of bent steel. The metal scraped over the habitat, leaving deep scratches in the paintwork. Casey moved up to help; no point in making more holes.

Together, they heaved the wreckage aside. A pocket of trapped air erupted towards the surface like a fart bubble in a giant's bathtub. Casey waved the dirt away from the shell. The wreckage had cut through the sphere's aluminum cladding and the section underneath had flooded. He made a note that Sphere 4 was damaged beyond repair. He had tried to access that sphere from inside, and almost drowned them all.

Tapping Tyler on the shoulder, Casey indicated they should move on. Sphere 3 appeared to be airtight, though the communications array in the central spire had fallen across it. Tyler lifted a six-foot long aluminum tube. It housed one of the sensor antennas which had snapped clean off the base when the entire assembly went over.

Casey spoke into the microphone in his respirator. "Stop fucking around."

The younger man saluted him with the pole and tossed it aside as they moved on to Sphere 2.

A steady stream of bubbles marked where the sphere had cracked. Casey swept the silt that had settled on the shell aside, clouding the water until he could see the gash in the metal.

"Got the patch?" he asked.

Tyler nodded. "*How much?*"

"Half-meter length should do it."

Tyler unrolled a length of matted fiberglass material and handed the trailing end to Casey. Using his dive knife, Tyler cut through the fabric and tucked the rest of the roll back into a dive bag on his belt.

The underwater epoxy came in a special aerosol can. Like an industrial strength can of shaving foam, it came out as a fast-setting resin for the fiberglass patch. The two divers worked over the split in the sphere; Casey holding the material against the surface while Tyler squeezed the adhesive out of its tube and used a palette knife to smooth it down.

After ten minutes, they pulled back and assessed their work.

"*Not bad aye, boss?*" Tyler had the cocky arrogance of youth. Casey nodded. Patching one leak didn't improve their survival chances by anything.

"Move on to the next one."

After they spent another five minutes lifting steel debris off it, Sphere 5 also proved to be undamaged. Casey watched the water around them for sharks while Tyler tossed the garbage off the roof.

"*Fuck!*" Tyler yelped. Casey twisted in the water, searching for any advancing threat. Tyler was stumbling backwards off the sphere's roof. In his wake, a broken corpse rose in the current and bobbed like an abandoned doll.

From the clothing, he was one of the engine room crew. Probably killed in the explosion, or drowned in the sudden flood of water that tore through the ship after the charges went off.

"Easy," Casey said. "He's dead. Nothing he can do to you now."

Tyler's breathing sounded ragged over the comms and Casey could see the whites of his eyes as he stared at the body.

"*This shit is fucked up.*"

"Tyler, stay focused. Look at me. Okay. Head back inside, I'll move him."

Tyler shook his head, "*Nah. I'm okay, aye. Just freaked me a little when he popped up.*"

Casey lifted the dead man by the shoulders and Casey took his feet. The body had a weird Jell-O-like quality to it. Lethal crush injuries or the pressure of the explosion had snapped most of his bones.

"On three, we hop down," Casey said.

*"Okay"*

"Three." Casey jumped and Tyler went with him. They floated down to the cold mud, sending small clouds puffing up when they landed.

"Put him over there." Casey nodded towards the darkness away from the habitat. The ocean would take care of the body in no time. Crabs, worms, fish, and even sharks would remove all trace in a week.

Moving with an awkward gait under the strange load, the two divers walked away from the habitat. Casey didn't want to lose sight of the structure and kept glancing back to make sure it was in view.

*"Look out!"* Tyler yelled. The body in Casey's hands jerked. He let go and leapt backwards. The sharks had come out of the darkness and the nearest one's massive teeth snapped on empty water as the body sank to the bottom.

"Move!" Casey yelled, his voice distorting the radio microphone in his helmet.

Tyler used his gloved hands and feet to propel himself in a rapid crawl away from the drifting corpse.

The sharks circled, homing in on the engineer's body and driving forward to snap chunks of the grey flesh. Casey felt a hot fury rising in his chest. *Fuckers.*

He pulled a dive knife from the sheath on his leg and pushed towards the nearest shark. The dense water resisted his slashing motion, but the knife caught the shark along the side behind its gills as it snapped at drifting scraps. The water darkened with blood. The shark convulsed, thrashing in the water and moving out of Casey's reach.

*Oh crap...* he passed into the drifting cloud of fresh blood and dropped into a crouch. The sharks were moving more rapidly, six, seven... all great whites. They weren't attacking each other, or hunting independently; they seemed to be working together, coming at their target from different directions, driving a couple of panicked fish ahead of them.

Casey turned on his feet, catching sight of a shark as it opened its mouth to take a chunk out of his shoulder. The diver jerked aside and stabbed upwards, the blade plunging deep into the shark's underbelly. The knife dragged out of Casey's hand as the fish leapt away with a flick of its long tail.

*"Boss! Come on!"* Tyler had returned to be within transmitting range for the dive radios. Casey scuttled backwards, keeping his back near the ocean bottom and watching above for attacking sharks.

Tyler was striding forward with the aluminum pole under his arm like a jousting lance. He thrust at an approaching shark. The end of the pole glance off the creature's sloping head and it quickly changed direction.

"I told you to get back inside!" Casey panted.

*"Can't, sharks are sniffing around the dive entrance."*

"The fuck?"

*"I reckon they can smell us and want a piece, aye?"*

"Sharks can smell really well, but that's in water."

*"They can't sniff out the girls inside, can they?"*

Casey wanted to say, *of course not.* Then he remembered something about sharks. "They can detect electrical fields. Like the kind generated by a fish hiding in the sand or behind some camouflaging seaweed. Or even peoples' heartbeats."

*"Here they come again."* Tyler was backing up and readying his aluminum pole. The sharks swam across the divers' view, keeping out of range, but moving to get behind them. Being stalked by predators that could come at you from almost any direction, even directly overhead, made seeing them coming challenging.

*"What do we do?"* Tyler sounded close to panic. He jabbed the pole at a shark, which simply swam out of reach and continued circling.

"Follow me," Casey said and marched away from the habitat. Tyler hesitated and then followed.

For Casey, the idea of climbing out of the water while the sharks were closing in made his toes curl and his balls shrink up to his armpits.

The sharks closed in as the two divers strode across the ocean floor. A few jabs from Tyler's aluminum pole sent them veering away as the wreck of the *Waitangirua* loomed out of the darkness. Even broken, the ship towered over the two divers. Tyler stared in awe at the fallen vessel. It felt weird seeing it here on the bottom, as dead as a beached whale.

Casey climbed up the hull, walking over the dull painted

surface as if he were hiking over a low hill. Tyler took one last look around in the darkness and then added some air to his buoyancy vest so he could float up to join his boss.

They paused at a gaping hole torn in the side of the ship below the waterline. *It's ironic,* Casey thought. *Now the entire ship is below the water line.*

*"Wreck diving used to be fun,"* Tyler said.

"Be extremely careful. We don't know if there are any more explosives or what other hazards are now loose."

Tyler thought that sharks were probably pretty high on the hazard list right now. Being inside a wreck could only be safer.

"We're looking for the waterproof batteries, cables, and anything that could be used to generate an electric current," Casey explained.

*"Sure thing, boss."* Tyler dipped his head into the wide opening in the ship's steel skin. Inside the hull, everything was pulverized or broken. He deflated his vest and slid deeper, watching for jagged edges and sharp points.

Casey went in feet first, sinking slowly as he turned to scan the dark water. A shark bite on his ass was not how he wanted this dive to end.

# CHAPTER 11

*Chatham Rise South Pacific Ocean, Longitude 44° S, Latitude 176° W. 400 meters below the surface.*

With their headlamps illuminating the destruction, Casey led the way deeper into the ship. The fuel tanks hadn't ruptured and here, deep in the guts of the ship, the water was mostly free of oil. They reached a steel pressure door, one of the bulkheads intended to protect the rest of the ship if the lower level flooded.

"Slowly…" Casey warned. Tyler took a grip on the locking wheel, and working together, they twisted it to the open position. The door cracked open, water at equal pressure on both sides allowed it to swing out of the frame. They continued through the ship, both divers taking note of the way back to the only exit they had.

Torn paper, food scraps, and plastic floated through the dark water. Everything moved on the currents, creating shadows that lunged and receded in the shifting lamplight.

Casey knew that the supplies he needed would be in a waterproof locker, near the deck level of the ship. He could have directed Tyler to swim to the deck side of the wreck, but there were opportunities to find things they could use inside, too.

The divers collected loose items as they went; a waterproof flashlight, though the lens had cracked; a folded plastic tarpaulin still bound up in a strap. In the corridor that ran past the galley, Casey found a small avalanche of tinned food that had spilled across the floor.

*"Aww, man, beans?"* Tyler almost sounded like he was grinning over the comms.

"Yeah, high in fiber and protein. If you need to fart, you can go the hell outside."

The younger diver seemed as resilient as a rubber band. Even in the face of near-certain death, he bounced back to frat-boy humor and fart jokes. The feeling that Tyler kept his spirits up by trusting that Casey would get them all out of this alive, turned the older man's stomach to churning acid.

A check on their remaining air-supply indicated they had about twenty minutes of safe dive time left. Casey bagged the cans and indicated to his dive computer. "Watch your air."

Tyler nodded and checked his own readout.

They crept through the twisted wreckage of the stricken ship the chaos of the explosions and the sinking were settling and everything still gleamed under their lights. Soon enough, the sea would start the long colonization process. Like the jungle covering an ancient city, the sea would cover the wreck with worms, silt, and the shells of animals that would live and die on the ship.

The way to what would have been the deck had opened in a

ragged tear with the steel hull torn open. The two divers emerged to float next to the deck that now stood like a cliff next to them.

"*We should get back, eh?*" Tyler said.

"Two more minutes, there's something I want to check."

Casey made his way along the wall of the deck. It felt eerie to have the deck that he had walked on now turned on its side. He stopped at a hole where the first of the two submersibles had been stored. The entire vehicle had gone, torn to pieces by the explosives dropped into the compact cabin.

Turning slowly, Casey noted that the second sub was missing from its anchor point. There were no signs of a second explosion, and he slowly sank down towards the starboard rail that rested against the silt of the ocean floor.

"*Chief?*"

"Follow me down if you can, Tyler; stay close and keep an eye out for sharks."

The second submersible had tumbled off the deck and now lay on its side less than twenty feet away from the wreck. Casey made a conscious effort to slow his breathing. If the sub had survived, and could be salvaged, it might be what they needed to get them to safety.

The heavy-duty plastic tarpaulin that protected the submersible from the sun and elements when it was safely stored on deck, floated like a cape in the water, a corner of it pinned under the sub.

With a cold hand, Casey swept the silt away from the clear bubble and peered into the sub's Perspex and steel cabin. An orange plastic container, about the size of a lunchbox lay on the pilot's seat. For whatever reason, it hadn't detonated like the other bombs. Getting it out would be suicidal, but then, so would staying down here until their air ran out.

Tyler's hand waved in Casey's peripheral vision. He gestured at his dive computer and the numbers were flashing red.

*"Time to go."*

Casey signaled okay, and with an eye out for hunting sharks, they made their way up and over the prone hulk. The dark water felt eerily empty the closer they got to the habitat. With no sign of sharks, Casey's nerves cranked up a notch. The predator you couldn't see was the one that may well be hunting you.

Turning slowly, the divers arrived at the entrance portal under the habitat. From here, it was a simple matter of swim up a few feet and climb out into the dive chamber.

"You go first," Casey said into his comms mask.

*"Age before beauty,"* Tyler replied. *"C'mon, man, it's getting cold."*

Casey didn't bother arguing. The kid was tired and chilled to the bone. In a few minutes, they could both be getting a hot drink and some dry clothes. Casey inflated his vest and rose upwards, breaching the surface with a slight splash. He climbed out of the water, using the short ladder bolted to the deck to get up.

Shedding his mask, BCD, weightbelt, and tanks, Casey turned to help Tyler as he breached the surface.

"Give me your weight-belt," Casey ordered.

Tyler dropped his hands, working the clip to release the belt. The water rippled around him and he looked at Casey, his eyes wide and bulging in terror behind his mask.

The shark took him around the legs, slamming Tyler against the rim of the dive portal. Casey heard Tyler's head crack against the frame and then he vanished, the shark dragging him out of the chamber.

"Tyler!" Casey dropped to his knees, scanning the blood-clouded water for any sign.

The rippling surface shattered as a flat grey head burst into the room. Casey yelled, throwing himself backwards as the shark's jaws snapped the air. The fish sank out of sight, leaving Casey pressed up against the dive chamber wall, shivering with cold and shock.

# CHAPTER 12

*Chatham Rise South Pacific Ocean, Longitude 44° S, Latitude 176° W. 400 meters below the surface.*

"Casey? Casey?" Aroha shook his arm. The diver was staring, unblinking at the water. "We heard you scream. Where's Tyler?"

"I should have sent him up first," Casey whispered.

"Oh, shit…" Aroha looked at the water. The blood had faded now, swept away by the constant currents. "You couldn't do anything."

"We should bring him in here, get him warm. He will be in shock." Nari stood in the open doorway to the inner chamber, her arms folded across her chest.

"Right." Aroha moved around Casey and helped him stand up. His skin felt cold to her touch and he started to shiver.

"He looked right at me."

Aroha couldn't tell if Casey was referring to Tyler or the shark.

"Come inside, we'll get you warmed up."

The women sealed the door to the dive chamber and stripped

Casey out of his drysuit. He didn't argue as they guided him to one of the narrow bunks and wrapped him in blankets.

"Can you heat some soup?" Aroha asked Nari. The Indian scientist drifted away to the tiny galley without comment.

"Sub," Casey muttered.

"What?"

He tried again, speaking between shivering convulsions. "Sub. On the wreck. Way to-to the surface. Slow decom-decompression."

"I thought you said they were blown up?"

"Bo-bomb didn't go off. It's-s-still sitting there. Sub-ub could go-go easy."

"Holy shit," Aroha breathed.

"Pro-problem," Casey managed. "Only room for t-two."

"So the others wait here, while the other two surface and raise the alarm. We get a rescue ship out here and we all go home and laugh about this in a year's time."

Casey closed his eyes. His feet and hands were burning as the blood flowed back into them. "Long time…" he whispered. "Too long."

Aroha watched him slip into sleep. He had barely rested since they came down here. With the shock and the cold, he was exhausted.

"Soup," Nari announced.

"Thanks. He's asleep," Aroha replied. Nari shrugged and warmed her hands around the plastic mug. After a moment of silence, she set the cup down on the floor and retreated to her blanket nest.

Aroha pulled a blanket off the top bunk and wrapped it around her shoulders. She sat in the cold chamber that was silent except for the occasional creak of the steel frame.

Without power coming down from the surface, the batteries would die in a few more hours and they would get unbearably cold. Without the regular infusion of fresh air from a surface supply, the filters would struggle to keep the oxygen content at a safe level. Without electricity, they would have no way to distill fresh water from salt. With limited food, they would die of hunger even if they managed to stay hydrated.

So far, the entire crew of the *Waitangirua*, the research team's engineer and most experienced divers, and now Tyler had died. Billy remained unconscious, which left three people with a vote. Casey was the only one with the skills and experience to pilot the tiny submersible safely. Which meant that either Nari or Aroha wouldn't be making the trip home.

Aroha turned her head; Nari had curled up into her blanket nest, but her eyes were open and watching Aroha. The other woman's stare made her uncomfortable. *How much of what Casey said about the sub had Nari heard?*

The sound of water dripping punctuated the stillness. Aroha stood up, shedding her blanket and went to check on the leaks. Water still trickled down the curving walls of the habitat's central chamber. She cautiously tapped on the exposed beams and heard a dull vibration. The ruptured spheres around them were nearly full of water. If the seals between them and the life support systems were damaged, then the lights would go out sooner than expected.

Claustrophobia whispered at the edges of Aroha's mind. She tried not to think about how trapped she felt. An entire ocean pressing down on them and sharks that displayed skilled pack-hunting skills actively trying to kill them. *Conserve energy,* Aroha told herself. She retreated to a vacant bunk and wrapped herself in the cold blankets. The rising moisture in the atmosphere hadn't soaked into the blankets yet, but when it did, the damp would suck the heat right out of her body and hypothermia would follow.

Shivering with more than the incessant cold, Aroha closed her eyes and willed herself to sleep.

Sometime later, a deep metallic groaning snapped her awake. Aroha strained to hear the source of the sound. She heard the dull *punk* of rivets popping and the soft wail of aluminum folding in on itself echo through the structure. Ruptured by debris and cracking under the pressure of the ocean, one of the support spheres had collapsed.

The trickling sound of water flowing into the habitat sounded louder, too. Aroha rolled off the bunk and gasped when her feet plunged into icy seawater. The water level washed over her toes and seemed to be rising steadily. The crack in the habitat sphere had lengthened, allowing more water to pour into their cramped living space.

"Casey, Nari!" Aroha splashed through the room, light items floating past her shoes.

Nari sat up on her bunk. "What's wrong?" she called.

"We're taking on water." Aroha headed towards the hairline crack in the foam insulation. Water was pouring down the curved wall now in a steady flow.

"It's okay," Casey said. "We can seal the crack and increase the air pressure. Force the water out again."

"Which is fine," Aroha countered. "Unless in doing that we put too much pressure on the compromised hull and it completely fails."

"You got a better idea?" Casey asked.

Aroha couldn't think of any right now. As long as the life support systems stayed online, they could effect a repair.

"Which sphere collapsed?" Casey asked, probing the sodden foam on the wall with his fingertips.

"I... don't know. The noise of it woke me up," Aroha said.

"Nari!" Casey yelled over his shoulder. "Check on the air filters and electronics. Don't touch anything; we can't risk you being electrocuted."

Nari crawled off the bunk and splashed through the ankle deep water. Back on shore, she had studied the plans and systems of the habitat with her usual attention to detail and twisted the plastic locking handles into the open position.

Behind the metal cover, digital read-outs and analog meters reported on gas levels, battery reserves remaining, and the status of the electrical systems.

Nari's gaze flicked over the systems and she took a deep breath. "Ahh... air filters have twenty-percent remaining. They will need changing out in a couple of hours. Electrics are still online. Emergency battery reserves are in the green. Everything else is—" Nari stopped midsentence as the electric system shorted out and the room went dark.

"I guess the power is out," she said.

"Back-up batteries, they were good right?" Casey called out in the dark.

"Yes, eight hours of minimal light and air scrubbing."

Aroha breathed slowly, given the rate the water was flooding into the sphere, they would drown in less than eight hours.

"Why won't the emergency lights come on?" Nari's voice cracked in the darkness.

"Nari," Aroha tried to keep her voice calm. "Give it a moment. Remember, the system has to switch over. If there is too much damage, the lights will never come on."

"We need to get out of here!" Nari cried out as she stumbled in the dark.

A weak glow filled the chamber as the emergency lighting system came on; it was barely enough to see by, but enough to banish the terrifying darkness.

"We have to get the sub running," Casey said.

"You said there is only room for two," Aroha whispered.

"I know. I can't make that decision. Maybe you and Nari can get to the surface, take it slow, and let the depressurization happen at a safe rate."

"No, we all have to get out," Aroha pleaded.

"It will not happen," Casey said, his eyes locked on hers.

"Fuck," Aroha said, clenching her fists and fighting back a scream of frustration.

"Yeah." Casey nodded. "Come on, I need you and Nari to help me with the sub. We need to salvage some stuff from the hab and use it to get the sub running."

"Nari?" Aroha shouted. "Suit up; we are going to the wreck."

"What? Why?" Nari had retreated to the top bunk.

"We need to get the submersible running, Casey needs our help."

Nari hesitated for a moment then nodded and slid down to the floor. "What about him?" She waved at Billy, who still lay unconscious on a narrow bunk.

"We do what we can to save those of us who are still walking," Casey said. Freezing saltwater showered down as the outer shell of the habitat cracked under the pressure.

Aroha and Nari went to the dive chamber, the changing air pressure making their ears pop.

No one wanted to sit on the edge of the open portal with their feet hanging in the dark water while they put on the BCD's, tanks, and weightbelts. It made the final dive preparations challenging in the cramped space.

The women went through the dive-buddy safety checks for the gear. Aroha stared into her friend's face and hoped the terror she saw in her eyes wasn't a reflection of her own fear.

"All okay?" Casey ducked through the low doorway and scrambled into his own drysuit.

"Checked and ready to go," Aroha replied.

"Nari?" Casey asked.

"I'm ready."

Casey geared up in a smooth process of actions. Every step was essential and part of the routine. He could do this with his eyes closed. Giving the girls an OK hand signal, he nodded when they returned it.

Stepping to the edge, Casey switched on the halogen flashlight he carried and tried not to think about Tyler. The kid's final moments would haunt him always. Right now though, they needed to get out of here and stay alive.

With a final exhale into the air, Casey stepped out into the portal and plunged downwards.

# CHAPTER 13

*Chatham Rise South Pacific Ocean, Longitude 44° S, Latitude 176° W. 400 meters below the surface.*

Casey landed a few seconds later on the silt under the habitat. Turning quickly, he scanned the dark water for sharks. Nothing moved. He kept turning, his skin crawling in near panic at how exposed he suddenly felt.

Nari dropped behind him, and he gave her an OK signal. She returned it and then Aroha sank into view. Casey checked she was OK before indicating they should follow him out into the abyssal darkness.

Casey wondered if the storm he had seen coming up from the south now raged on the surface, sucking the energy out of the ocean and dropping the temperature by a noticeable degree even at this depth. Casey told himself that was why he shivered and not the lurking terror of the sharks.

Reaching the broken hull of the *Waitangirua*, Casey motioned the two scientists forward.

"Can you hear me?" he asked.

*"Loud and clear,"* Aroha replied.

"Nari?" Casey stepped forward and adjusted a waterproof knob on the side of her helmet. "Can you hear me now?"

*"Yes."* Nari's voice sounded flat and distant. Casey stared into the clear Perspex of her helmet. He couldn't see her expression, but the whites of her eyes almost glowed against her dark complexion.

"We need to go up." Casey indicated the rising bulk of twisted steel behind them. "The sub is on the deck."

He let Nari go first, helping her to fill her BCD with some of her air-supply until the positive buoyancy helped lift her off her feet.

"Don't go up too far or too fast. Control your ascent," Casey said to Aroha. She nodded and her inflatable vest filled with air. Casey inflated his own BCD and swam up the face of the stricken ship.

They reached the rail, Aroha swimming hard and grabbing hold before remembering to let the air out of her BCD to equalize her buoyancy. Nari floated on upwards, her body still as she rose.

Casey kicked hard with his fins. Catching up with Nari, he grabbed her around the ankles and she screamed loud enough to make him wince.

"Nari! It's okay! You can't surface! You will die!"

*"I'm going to die anyway!"* she started sobbing. *"Let me go!"*

"I will do everything I can to get you to safety. I promise."

Casey climbed up the woman's body as they continued to ascend. He fumbled with numb fingers to release air from her

BCD. A stream of bubbles erupted from the vest and they began to sink again. With one arm around Nari, Casey managed his own vest, controlling their descent.

Aroha's helmet lights pierced the gloom, scanning the dark water like spotlights during an air raid. The two divers sank into view, the hi-vis colors of their BCD's catching the light.

"Nari, are you okay?" Aroha reached out a hand to steady her friend on the sloping deck.

"We need to keep moving." Casey's dive computer said that the internal heating system in his suit was malfunctioning. It might be a loose wire, or a dead battery. Either way, he was feeling the encroaching effect of the chill on his skin.

He led them down the face of the deck towards the starboard rail and the mini-sub that had survived the murderous sabotage of Vlok and his mercenaries.

The sub hadn't moved in the hours since Casey and Tyler had first discovered it. Now, Casey took time to examine the small vessel more carefully. There were no signs of damage beyond a few scrapes on the paintwork. The sub's design meant it could survive all manner of violent impacts and encounters at great depths. Getting inside without destroying it would be their greatest challenge.

The cockpit looked even smaller now; it would be physically impossible for three people to fit inside. Even if they did, the life-support systems that filtered air and kept the temperature bearable would not hold up to the extra body.

"Okay, this is what we are—" Casey started talking as he turned to address the two women. They had vanished.

"Aroha? Nari?" Casey turned slowly, staring into the murk, looking for any sign of the divers' lights. "Can you hear me?" The comms remained dead.

Something heavy clanked against the rising wall of the ship's deck. Casey pushed himself forward, crossing the space between the sub and the deck in long strides. A swirl of silt echoed around a diver's weight belt. The heavy lead bricks on a belt of thick webbing helped counteract the natural buoyancy of the diver and their suit. Without it, either Nari or Aroha were on their way to the surface and a painful death as the sudden change in pressure expanded the gases dissolved in their blood.

Casey sent a burst of air into his BCD and swam upwards. He used handholds on the deck to push himself up faster. Then, through the gloom, he saw a wavering helmet light. Surging forward, Casey swam up, releasing the air in his BCD at the last moment to bring him to a stationary position, level with Aroha.

She was hanging upside down, her feet waving towards the distant surface as she held on for dear life to the railing on the ship's upper-most side.

"Aroha, hang on!" Casey grabbed her vest and released the last of the air out of it. It wouldn't stop her floating away, but it might tip the balance in his favor to let him bring her down to her lost belt.

"You need to help me, swim hard. Straight down."

*"I can't."* Aroha's breath came in ragged gasps, close to complete panic.

"Look at me." Casey pushed his face close to her mask. "Breathe... in... hold it... and out... breathe in... hold it... out...

slowly. That's it."

Casey reached up and pulled Aroha's legs down until she lay parallel to the rail.

"Grip with your legs and your arms. Wrap yourself around the railing." He pushed her stiff limbs into position. Soon, Aroha clung to the rail like a giant starfish.

"I'm going to retrieve your weight belt. I will be back in one minute."

"*Nari, she attacked me. Be careful,*" Aroha spoke in an adrenalized whisper.

Casey flipped over and swam down to the bottom, exhaustion burning his lungs as he sank into the cold silt.

The lead ingots of the weight-belt dragged on his arms. Casey's BCD inflated and he started up the cliff-face of the stricken ship's deck. If Nari had flipped out, completely lost her fucking mind, then she might be already dead.

The blade of a knife glinted in the edge of Casey's helmet lights. He twisted towards the incoming blow. Nari slashed at his air-hose, the stainless steel blade in her hand cutting through the water with ease.

Casey grabbed Nari's wrist. Twisting her arm back, he avoided the knife. Her other hand grabbed at Casey's mask. He felt the soft rubber of his respirator hose squeeze shut in her grip. He tried to inhale and it felt like inhaling mud.

Nari and Casey grappled in the freezing dark. Everything twisted around as they tumbled over each other. Casey swung the weight-belt over his head and felt it impact hard on Nari's helmet. She let go of his air hose and the lights of her helmet washed over him as Nari vanished upwards into the darkness, leaving Casey struggling to catch his breath.

"Wait…" Casey mumbled. He floated up, swimming hard, desperate to reach Aroha.

Nari reached Aroha first and she slashed with the knife. Nari's knife skills were amateur, which meant she could kill Aroha in seconds.

The two women danced around each other, Nari stabbing and slicing through the water while Aroha clung to the rail and tried to avoid her by scuttling crab-like along the metal frame.

Casey rocketed into the midst of the fight. When he came close enough to be in comms range, he started yelling. "Nari! Wait! I can get you out of here! I can save you!"

Nari screamed a savage and maddened shriek. Aroha was sobbing, making wordless and desperate noises. Casey ignored the sudden beep of his dive computer, warning him that he was down to the reserve of his air-supply.

The Indian woman twisted past Casey. She grabbed Aroha's air hose and cut through it with a sharp slicing motion. Casey's vision clouded in a surge of uncontrolled bubbles. Aroha threw herself aside and slammed into the rail.

Nari backed off, abandoning them to their fate as Casey reached for Aroha. He pulled her against his chest and started swimming. The respirators were built into the hard shell of their helmets. He had no way to share his air with Aroha. Even the emergency respirator hose wouldn't work if he couldn't get air inside her helmet.

The habitat now remained as their only hope for another

chance at survival. Aroha thrashed against Casey when he hit the silt of the ocean floor.

Running hard across the hard, grey surface, he pulled Aroha with him. Panicked convulsions wracked her as she fought against the inevitable.

"Hold on," Casey hissed. The chances of resuscitating her depended on too many factors for him to fathom. An entire emergency room of trained doctors and nurses might be able to bring her back.

The lights of the habitat flickered in the gloom. The sharks swimming through the shafts of light created random strobe patterns that just added to Casey's overwhelming despair.

Aroha shuddered and went still. "Hang on..." Casey whispered. His gaze swept around as they reached the crushed spheres of the dying hab. Dozens of sharks were now snatching morsels from the drifting scraps of torn bodies drifting on the dark currents.

With Aroha in his arms, Casey walked the remaining hundred yards. Quicksilver shapes flitted in the darkness a circling storm of cold savagery that Casey had no defense against.

"Just fucking try it, you bastards."

Passing under the habitat exposed him to the worst moments of pure terror. With no way of seeing if the predators were closing in on him or not, he pushed Aroha's body up into the dive chamber. With a final look around, Casey leapt up and dragged himself into the steel sphere.

# CHAPTER 14

*Chatham Rise South Pacific Ocean, Longitude 44° S, Latitude 176° W. 400 meters below the surface.*

Ripping his helmet off, Casey sucked a lungful of salt-tainted air. Rolling over, he unclipped Aroha's helmet and pulled her mask away. Sealing her mouth with his, he pushed a deep breath into her lungs.

Moving to his knees, Casey pressed hard on Aroha's chest. A regular pumping rhythm would hopefully push the blood cooling in her veins through her heart and lungs. "Come on, live!" He huffed air into Aroha again then resumed the chest compressions. This shouldn't work. A voice in the back of his mind reminded him of the grim statistics a paramedic once told him. Less than twenty percent of people survived a resuscitation attempt like this. Most of them never fully recovered.

He worked her chest again and leaned over to give her another gust of oxygen. Aroha jerked and coughed. A sour mix of bile and phlegm splattered on her lips.

"Aroha!" Casey yelled. Twisting her onto her side, he pounded her back while she coughed and gasped for air.

"Fuck," she moaned.

"You're okay. You're okay." Casey was laughing. He collapsed onto the steel grille floor.

"Nari...?" Aroha whimpered from her fetal position on the floor. Her chest heaved in the confines of the dry-suit and her face had the same bleached pallor as her hair.

Casey got to his feet and tried not to fall over at the sudden dizziness. "We have to get the other tanks. The hab isn't going to last long."

"I need a minute." Aroha waved him away.

"Right. No problem." Casey pulled the last of the Trimix tanks from the rack. There were slots for two respirator hoses to attach to the primary regulator. That meant they could both take air from the one source. He set to work, unscrewing the caps and setting the hoses in place. His numb hands made the job a thousand times harder than it should be.

"Where is Nari?" Aroha asked.

"She didn't make it." Casey didn't look up. He couldn't try to explain right now. He wasn't sure he knew the truth himself yet.

"Did the sharks get her?" Aroha shivered with cold and horror.

They would eventually; it would do as the truth for now. "I guess," Casey replied.

Bubbles ruptured the surface of the dive portal. Nari sprang out of the water and slammed her knife, point first, into the steel grille, the blade cutting through the hard rubber of Aroha's fin, pinning her foot to the floor. "Casey!" Aroha screamed.

Casey lunged forward as Nari scrambled out of the water. "You were going to leave me to die!" Nari's snarl was muffled through the heavy padding of her dive mask. "You were going to let us all die!"

"No!" Casey raised his hands. "I was trying to get you both on the sub!"

Nari pulled the knife out and slashed at Casey. The tight neoprene suit slowed the strike. Casey shoved the woman hard. Pushing her back against the door to the flooded habitat.

"Nari, calm the fuck down!"

Nari unclipped her helmet and let it fall to the floor. "You tried to kill me," she insisted.

The door behind her cracked open sending a surge of seawater gushing into the small chamber. The flood swept Nari off her feet, sending her rolling towards the portal and the cold ocean.

Casey thrust out his hand and grabbed Aroha's arm as she washed passed. Pulling her to safety, he helped her stand against the rising flood.

Billy appeared in the open doorway. The water pouring out of the ruptured habitat sphere had already risen halfway up his thighs.

The habitat creaked and groaned. A moment later, the pressure change became too much for the damaged structure and the main sphere ruptured. Water exploded through the open doorway. Billy clung to the frame with one hand and grabbed Nari by the wrist. She screamed and stabbed Billy in the thigh as he pulled her against him.

Casey slung the last of the Trimix tanks onto his shoulders and slid the helmet over Aroha's head. "Breathe!" he yelled over the roaring water. She inhaled as he secured his own dive helmet.

Billy gripped Nari in a bear hug even as she struggled and stabbed at him. His calm stare caught Casey's wild eyes and he nodded slowly.

Casey hesitated for a moment then nodded back. With an arm wrapped around Aroha, he dropped through the dive portal. The space above them folded in on itself like origami.

Around them, blood filled the water in an expanding cloud, dark and bitter as ink.

"*Nari!*" Casey screamed.

"She's gone!" Casey staggered backwards, dragging Aroha with him out from under the crumpling habitat. Intact, it could have stood at this depth for a hundred years. Punctured and crushed, water tore through the interior spaces with an explosive force.

Aroha swallowed her gasping tears. "*Sharks*," she warned and twisted out of Casey's numb grip. They both pulled dive knives from sheaths on their belts. They circled slowly, watching each other's backs as the silver shapes slipped out of the darkness, drawn by the fresh blood filling the water.

Ducking under a charging fish, Aroha noted the flaps under its smooth, grey belly. *Male,* she thought automatically. The appendages, called claspers, allowed the male to grip the female during mating. Mating behavior in great whites was still one of the great mysteries of the world's oceans. The only thing that Aroha was certain of, females could be much larger than males.

The fish they had seen around the wreck of the *Waitangirua* and the habitat were males, ten to fourteen feet long, which made them average sharks. The organized and cooperative pack-hunting tactics they had shown were not unheard of, but suggested an intelligence far beyond that normally taken for granted.

The sharks came from the left and right. Arching their backs, they threw their heads back in the last moment as they bared their teeth to bite. Aroha ducked under the torpedo shaped body. She didn't want to add to the blood in the water by cutting or stabbing any of the charging sharks. A good smack on the nose would usually send a shark away, the equivalent of kicking a man in the balls, her biology professor had once said.

Casey jabbed a twelve-footer in the face with his knife. The shark convulsed, twisting away with a trickle of blood streaming from the cold flesh of its nose. "Keep moving!" Casey shouted over the comms.

Aroha danced over the hard-packed silt as the sharks swam over them, the cold patience of their movement chilling her more than the dark waters.

"Look out!" Casey lunged and stabbed a shark dropping like a hunting bird towards Aroha from above. Now, at least a dozen silent predators slipped in and out of their view as more sharks emerged from the darkness.

"Keep moving," Aroha said. Her chest ached from the CPR and her throat burned from the bile she had vomited up.

Casey strode along the ocean floor, turning constantly, scanning the perimeter marked by the beam from his helmet lights. Aroha hurried with him, bound close by the shared Trimix air supply. The sooner they got to the wrecked ship, the better chance they had of finding cover and maybe, just maybe, getting to the safety of the tiny sub.

Casey's helmet lights dimmed. Aroha pushed herself to move faster, afraid that he was getting ahead. Then the light dimmed further and he was within arm's reach. Casey raised a gloved hand and slapped the side of his helmet. The light flickered and went out. The darkness rushed in and the water felt even colder.

"Can you hear me?" Aroha asked over the comms. Casey turned and tapped his helmet and then made a shaking gesture with one fist.

*No.*

"Shit," Aroha whispered. The batteries on Casey's suit had run out or malfunctioned. He had no heating, except the thin layer of air between the thick neoprene suit and his skin. He had no lights and no radio. The air supply was entirely regulated by the pressure in the tanks, so they would not run out of air just yet. Aroha swallowed hard against the barbed wire in her throat. The terror of her suffocation would haunt her forever.

Casey took her arm and they marched on. The debris field around the wrecked ship told them they were getting closer. They picked their way over magazines and scraps of cloth that waved in the gentle breeze of the currents.

Pieces of metal and broken machines slowed them down. They worked their way carefully over the largest chunks and either walked around or stepped over anything smaller.

In her head, Aroha heard the old Police song, *Walking On The*

*Moon.* The bottom of the sea felt just as alien and deadly. Neil Armstrong was just as far from help, but at least he didn't have to worry about sharks trying to kill him as he took his small step.

*Focus,* she reminded herself. The constant watch for incoming sharks and the treacherous ground underfoot were more than enough to keep her attention from wavering. *Some kind of shock,* Aroha decided. *Or hypoxia.* The shortage of oxygen for several minutes had no doubt fried her brain.

Casey tackled Aroha a moment before a large great white swam past. The beast's gaping maw passed within inches of her face. She tried to scream as the shark twisted its sinuous body and renewed the attack. Aroha pressed herself against Casey, until were both lying with their backs to the cold sand. Now, they had nowhere to go and no way to avoid the savage assault.

The shark jerked under a jarring impact and then rolled away. The head of the twelve-foot male shark spun slowly through the water, trailing a thick cloud of blood and flecks of tissue. The jaws that had bitten the shark completely in half were at the business end of the biggest shark Aroha had ever seen.

A massive body swam past, and kept going as Casey counted the passing seconds. He estimated the beast was at least forty feet long. *Forty feet?* That wasn't a shark. That was something out of a horror film.

Aroha barely breathed as she stared in wonder. *Alpha shark,* she thought. A massive great white, big enough to swallow other sharks whole. The new arrival had to be female; the males of the species didn't get that big. There had been stories, a tagged great white had vanished, and when her tag washed up on a beach a few months later, the data suggested she had been swallowed whole by something of unimaginable size. The theories ranged from giant squid to Cthulhu, the pulp-horror monstrosity created in the 1930's by H.P. Lovecraft.

Most shark researchers agreed that the best candidate for the loss of the tagged shark was a truly massive shark. Aroha saw now that it could be true. Here, in the cold waters off the coast of New Zealand, where sharks were believed to come and breed, a monster of Biblical proportions now swept through the teeming swarm of sharks. The colossal female took a fleeing male in two quick bites. The first bite severed him behind the dorsal fin; the second snap swallowed what remained.

# CHAPTER 15

*Chatham Rise South Pacific Ocean, Longitude 44° S, Latitude 176° W. 400 meters below the surface.*

Casey scrambled to his feet, dragging Aroha upright. She saw his eyes were wide and terrified in the white glare of her helmet lights. A strange calmness had fallen over the researcher. She knew where she wanted to direct her energies next. She had seen living proof of an alpha shark. Perhaps a freak of nature inflicted with gigantism, or perhaps a super predator that had survived to reach this size by sheer luck and savagery.

Casey pulled Aroha against the high steel cliff of the ship's hull. He indicated upwards and she nodded before looking back at the dark water where the alpha might still be terrorizing her smaller brethren. Aroha silently vowed that she would see the creature again, study it and learn if there could be others, perhaps even larger, somewhere in the almost endless darkness of the world's seas.

With a whoosh of gas, the two divers' BCDs filled and lifted them off the floor of the ocean. They rose steadily, managing their ascent like hot-air ballooners, letting the air out until they slipped over the ship's rail and began their descent down the torn deck.

By now, neither of them could feel their fingers and toes. Aroha wondered how Casey could cope with the cold that was creeping through her heated suit. When she saw his face, it was pale to the point of being grey. She couldn't see his lips, but guessed they were blue by now.

Arm in arm, they touched down next to the mini-sub. Casey made a complicated series of gestures and hand signals. Aroha replied with an exaggerated shrug, his message completely meaningless to her.

Casey tried to think through the shivering twitches that wracked him. He was so cold he had lost feeling in his hands and feet. With the failure of his suit battery, he worried he would freeze to death before they got to safety.

Motioning her to stay put, he stumbled around the submersible and gathered in the floating tarpaulin. Coming back, he spread the dense plastic sheet over the top.

Aroha watched curiously as Casey cut slits in the corners and then as he struggled to tie the pieces securely around the struts at the bottom of the sub.

Realization dawned and Aroha crouched down, taking the tarpaulin and securing it around the steel legs.

It took her a minute to secure the two remaining corners. Now, the center of the tarpaulin pressed against the top of the sub and the sides were stretched tight down the machine's flanks.

Casey gestured at Aroha again, trying to communicate that he needed her to remove her BCD. The vest was the same as a life jacket, with bladders in it to hold air pumped in via the regulator hose.

Without creating a pocket of pressurized air, the interior of the submersible would flood. Casey hoped putting air into the cabin would keep the water pumped out. He also fervently hoped that the electronics inside were still secure behind their waterproof seals. Otherwise, they would die.

Aroha didn't understand his request, so he reached out and unclipped her BCD, then fumbled at the zipper. She helped slipping out of the device with a supple twist of her shoulders.

Using more of their precious air reserve, Casey filled the vest with gas until it swelled and strained to fly like a helium-filled balloon. *Stay,* he motioned and Aroha nodded.

Pushing the BCD under the tarpaulin, he pressed down on the valve and the tarpaulin vibrated under the sudden rush of trapped air.

The makeshift airlock barely inflated against the water pressure. Casey pumped more air into it, inflating the tarpaulin sack until it swelled enough to allow him to gesture at Aroha to go underneath it. He followed her a moment later they stood with their heads above water. Casey pushed Aroha.

Taking one last breath, Casey opened the valve on the Trimix tank and let the remaining air flow out in a hissing roar. The tarpaulin swelled, straining against the upward push of the air and pushing the water level down until the narrow access hatch was almost above the water line.

Casey unclipped his dive helmet and yanked it off.

"Open the hatch! Get inside!"

Aroha didn't hesitate. She removed her own helmet and handed it to Casey.

With trembling hands, she unfastened her weight belt and twisted the handle on the sub's access hatch. It opened and water started to pour inside.

Squirming through the hatch, she gave Casey an OK signal from the cramped cockpit. With numb hands, Casey disconnected his own BCD. Dropping the gear at his feet, he crawled inside the submarine and froze.

The orange plastic box, which looked strong enough to resist him trying to open it, waited on the floor of the cockpit. Swallowing hard, Casey picked it up with the same nut-crawling fear he would have if it were a live snake.

With a rising waterfall of freezing seawater pouring over the lip of the hatch as the air leaked out from the tarpaulin, Casey pushed the orange box out through the open door and heaved the hatch shut; spinning the locking handle until it sealed tight.

Water sloshed around their feet and the only sound they could hear was the chattering of their teeth.

Casey wriggled into the pilot seat as the half-inflated air sack quivered. The view through the Perspex hull of the cockpit erupted in an explosion of bubbles and tearing plastic. A shark ripped the covering away and snapped at the water, looking for the prey it could sense.

"We are safe in here, yeah?" Aroha had squeezed herself into the corner to give Casey room to maneuver.

"Yeah, should be." Casey tried to ignore the frenzied attack going on a few feet away. With a silent prayer to whichever gods may be watching, he activated the submarine's power systems. The control panel lit up and the whirr of the internal heating systems breathed warm air over them.

The sub's small bilge pump started and the water drained out of the cramped cabin.

"Get in this seat." Casey motioned for Aroha to sit beside him. She squirmed into position. "Hold on."

The submarine's propellers hummed into life, stirring up the silt around them. Slowly, they lifted off the bottom of the ocean. Aroha suppressed a whoop of delight. The shark tearing the tarpaulin to shreds swam away into the darkness as the strange metal beast rose up and turned to scan the wrecked ship.

The array of halogen lights illuminated the darkness, reflecting off the torn steel and grey silt. "We made it," Casey breathed.

Aroha started to reply, when her eyes went wide. The sub rocked under the force of a massive impact.

Casey wrestled with the controls, helpless under the sudden onslaught. Through the Perspex window, he could see a massive white shape.

"It's the alpha shark!" Aroha yelled. She struggled into the co-pilot's seat and snapped the 8-point harness into place.

"The what?"

"Alpha shark. Rare, giant, female great white," Aroha explained in as few words as possible.

"It's trying to eat us?" Casey couldn't quite believe it as the massive creature's teeth scraped over the steel hull.

"Probably. I mean, she can bite a regular fourteen footer in half. We're just another meal."

"Get off there, you bitch!" Casey shouted through the window.

The submersible swung around as the shark let go. A moment later, a gaping maw lined with triangular teeth bigger than Casey's hand opened and the front of the sub had a clear view into the darkness of the shark's gullet.

"She's gonna fucking swallow us?" Casey felt the sub's propellers whining as they strained against the obstruction.

"No, she's trying to bite us into smaller chunks. Shark's will bite anything to find out if it is edible. She'll give up—"

The shark bit down again, tearing one of the halogen lamps from its mounting. The light went out and the alpha tossed it down her throat.

Casey sent the submersible whirring backwards. The shark loomed large as she watched the strange fish fleeing. With a single sweep of the massive tail, the shark was on them again. The sub shuddered under the blow and tilted onto its side, the weight of the massive creature driving them down to the bottom again.

"Shit!" Casey yelled. Beside him, Aroha screamed as her head bounced off a steel panel in the tight space.

The shark released the sub and Casey worked the controls, bringing the machine back on an even keel.

"She's coming back!" Aroha yelled.

In the swirling mess of dark water and disturbed silt, a red light blinked. Casey glanced at Aroha; she had one hand pressed against the rising lump on the side of her head.

"Grab the joysticks in front of you. Just hold it steady."

Aroha looked confused, but did as he asked. Casey let go of the drive controls and seized a second set of smaller joysticks. He flicked the switches that activated the robotic arms used for collecting samples.

"Shiiiit!" Aroha yelled as the shark buffeted the sub again.

"Left hand forward, right hand back!" Casey shouted. Aroha twisted the drive controls and the sub turned sideways. The alpha shark slid past, a giant eye as dark as ebony stared at them as she went.

"Now, go forward, easy!" Casey ordered.

"What are you doing?" Aroha demanded.

"That red light, it's the last bomb from the ship. It didn't go off."

"This is no time to be collecting evidence!" Aroha yelled and twisted the controls. The alpha shark's mouth scraped over the Perspex window, leaving scratches in the hardened plastic.

"That explosive is counting down. Maybe the water pressure or something triggered it."

"So let's get out of here!" Aroha maneuvered the sub out of range as the shark bore down on them again.

"We can't get away from this fucking thing. Either it will tear us open, or it will drag us down."

Aroha wanted to tell Casey that the shark would realize they were inedible and would leave them alone. Why the creature hadn't already swum off in search of a less-armored meal was something she couldn't understand.

"Left... left... now straight, almost got it... Stop!" Casey watched intently as the mechanical arm reached out and the utility claw scraped over the orange casing of the bomb.

"How long?" Aroha asked, looking around for the shark.

"Uhhh... we're good." Casey blinked the salt water from his eyes. He could see the red numbers ticking over on the digital clock. Less than a minute until it blew them to pieces.

"Do you have it?" Aroha asked.

"Almost..."

"Christ, now I know how one of those horse things feels. You know, those Mexican ones."

"A piñata?" Aroha would have laughed at the idea, but in the choking grip of terror, she could barely breathe. "Hold on, she's trying again."

Casey's focus centered on the small square of orange resting on the silt. Aroha turned the submersible, but the shark was ready. Her cartilaginous skeleton twisted in a fraction of her body length and she rammed into the sub with the force of a runaway truck. The hull groaned, the skids grinding as they slid through the hard-packed silt.

"Goddamn bitch," Aroha snarled.

"Shake her off," Casey replied.

Aroha worked the controls, the submersible twisted and bounced in the grip of the shark's teeth. She let go and the sub spun in a flat circle. Casey jerked the robotic arm upwards. As they swept past the alpha shark, he pushed the arm forward. The plastic box hit her in the side of the mouth. The shark tossed its head and the red counter vanished into the gaping crevasse of her dark mouth.

The shark bit down and jerked left and right. The robotic arm tore off and the sub bounced off the bottom.

"Get us out of here, eh?" Casey said. Aroha pushed the controls forward. With her thumbs working to adjust the angle of the dive planes, the propellers surged. The sub powered up into the darkness.

"Level out!" Casey shouted. "We have to ascend slowly."

"Okay! Okay!" Aroha hunched over the controls, cringing as they waited for the destruction of the blast.

When the bomb detonated in the pulsing gullet of the alpha shark seven seconds later, the massive creature's body exploded in a rapidly moving cloud of blood and raw meat.

The shockwave expanded in all directions, rippling through the water. When the blast hit the sub, the two occupants rattled like stones in a tin can. The submersible jerked like it had been kicked. The lights flickered, and for a moment, Aroha was sure the electric engine would die and they would sink to the bottom again.

Casey strained to look behind the sub. On the edge of the circle of light, a feeding frenzy tore through the remains of the alpha shark.

"Fuck..." Casey muttered.

"We good?" Aroha asked.

"Yeah... I think every shark in the Pacific is back there." Casey sighed. "I think we are going to be okay."

"You sure?" In the aftermath of the adrenaline, Aroha's voice cracked.

"Hey, I'll drive if you like. Take a break." Casey worked the controls, adjusting pitch and speed, noting that the sub's batteries were fully charged, maybe enough for the long drive back to shore.

"How long till we can surface?" Aroha asked.

"The sub interior is pressurized to the same depth we are. We need to decompress slowly. So two, maybe three days?" Casey adjusted the sub's direction and pitch. By controlling the internal pressure, they could decompress slowly and reach the surface in about seventy-two hours.

"Can we survive that long?" Aroha asked.

"Sure, we have a recycling air system. Emergency rations, fresh water, and a toilet that will make you wish you'd held it."

"Okay. So the sub is on autopilot?"

"Not really; it's going in one direction at a steady, but very gradual rate of ascent. We just need to keep adjusting the atmospheric pressure every hour or so and keep an eye on each other for sign of decompression sickness. The good thing is by the time we surface, we should be within a few hundred yards of a New Zealand beach."

"So what else do we do for what, three days?"

"I spy?"

Aroha giggled, a strange sound in close atmosphere. Moving carefully, she turned until she was kneeling on her narrow seat. She unzipped the drysuit and peeled it off her upper body. Casey felt his mouth go dry.

"Well, there is something we could do to pass the time," Aroha breathed.

"Not much room," Casey croaked.

Aroha finished stripping naked and slid over until she was kneeling across his lap. "You've never done it in the front seat of a car?"

Casey shrugged, his reply lost in the sudden warmth of her kiss.

# CHAPTER 16

*Caroline Bay, Timaru, Longitude 44° S, Latitude 171° W.*

This early on a summer's morning, the Caroline Bay Park was deserted. The few dog walkers patrolling the beach greeted each other as they passed. The plastic grocery bags they carried to collect their pet's leavings gripped conscientiously in one hand.

Pausing to let her Shih Tzu, Mitzi, squat in the dark sand, Mildred Turnbull stared out at the waves. Something glinted out there in the early morning sun. Perhaps a kayak or maybe a whale? She took a deep breath and closed her eyes, Mitzi scratching the sand at the end of the leash.

The action of the waves pulsed as regular as a heartbeat. Mildred listened to the sea and felt the waves against the rhythm of her own heart. This daily meditation brought her closer to the earth and filled Mildred with a great sense of peace.

Mitzi jumped up and barked, dashing forward to the extent of her leash, growling and barking at the surf.

"Steady, Mitzi." Mildred remained focused on her morning meditation. Just her and the waves.

Mitzi whined, straining against the leash. She bounced, barking and growling.

"Really, Mitzi?" Mildred opened her eyes. The reflection vanished behind the breakers and then appeared again. It wasn't a kayak.

Moving closer, almost to the edge of the foaming residue left by each retreating wave, Mildred shaded her eyes and stared into the surf.

A strange craft crested an incoming wave, the propellers catching the air and whining with a surge in revolutions.

Mitzi barked in a frenzy, Mildred bent down and scooped her dog up. The small submarine churned the last wave and ran aground on the coarse sand.

A hatch cracked open and an unsteady hand emerged, waving carefully like a lizard's tongue tasting the air.

Mildred stared in open-mouthed astonishment as a young woman wearing some kind of wetsuit crawled out through the hatch. She dropped to her knees in the surf. Sweeping her hair back, she looked up at the sky and laughed.

A man now crawled out of the submarine. He straightened up and stretched. The woman squealed as a wave washed over her hips. Standing up, they hugged, and arms wrapped around each other's shoulders, they stumbled onto the beach.

"Hi," Aroha said, her voice rough after three days in the tiny sub.

"Good morning," Mildred replied. Mitzi whined in greeting.

Casey reached out and lifted the sipper bottle of water from Mildred's coat pocket. Without a word, he popped the top and tilted his head back, squirting water down his throat. When he stopped to gasp for air, Aroha almost snatched the bottle from his hand and drained the rest of it.

"Thank you," Casey croaked. "Timaru?" He indicated the buildings beyond the beach.

"Yes. Who are you? Where have you come from?" Mildred asked the first of the hundred questions she could think of.

"That is a long story," Aroha said. "One we would be happy to tell you over breakfast."

"I… oh." Mildred realized she was totally intrigued by the strange pair of castaways.

"We should contact the police," Casey said.

"Yes, but breakfast first," Aroha nodded. "I'm sorry. My name is Aroha, and this is Casey."

"There's a café not far from here. I enjoy a coffee there after my morning walk with Mitzi," Mildred explained.

"Great. We can tell you a great story over coffee and breakfast." Casey indicated that Mildred should lead the way.

Shaking her head, Mildred set Mitzi down and let the dog lead them on the familiar route to the café where a bowl of fresh water would be waiting.

# THE END

# CHECK OUT OTHER GREAT
# DEEP SEA THRILLERS

## THEY RISE
## by Hunter Shea

Some call them ghost sharks, the oldest and strangest looking creatures in the sea.

Marine biologist Brad Whitley has studied chimaera fish all his life. He thought he knew everything about them. He was wrong. Warming ocean temperatures free legions of prehistoric chimaera fish from their methane ice suspended animation. Now, in a corner of the Bermuda Triangle, the ocean waters run red. The 400 million year old massive killing machines know no mercy, destroying everything in their path. It will take Whitley, his climatologist ex-wife and the entire US Navy to stop them in the bloodiest battle ever seen on the high seas.

## SERPENTINE
## by Barry Napier

Clarkton Lake is a picturesque vacation spot located in rural Virginia, great for fishing, skiing, and wasting summer days away.

But this summer, something is different. When butchered bodies are discovered in the water and along the muddy banks of Clarkton Lake, what starts out as a typical summer on the lake quickly turns into a nightmare.

This summer, something new lives in the lake...something that was born in the darkest depths of the ocean and accidentally brought to these typically peaceful waters.

It's getting bigger, it's getting smarter...and it's always hungry.

# CHECK OUT OTHER GREAT DEEP SEA THRILLERS

## SEA RAPTOR
by John J. Rust

From terrorist hunter to monster hunter! Jack Rastun was a decorated U.S. Army Ranger, until an unfortunate incident forced him out of the service. He is soon hired by the Foundation for Undocumented Biological Investigation and given a new mission, to search for cryptids, creatures whose existence has not been proven by mainstream science. Teaming up with the daring and beautiful wildlife photographer Karen Thatcher, they must stop a sea monster's deadly rampage along the Jersey Shore. But that's not the only danger Rastun faces. A group of murderous animal smugglers also want the creature. Rastun must utilize every skill learned from years of fighting, otherwise, his first mission for the FUBI might very well be his last.

## OCEAN'S HAMMER
by D.J. Goodman

Something strange is happening in the Sea of Cortez. Whales are beaching for no apparent reason and the local hammerhead shark population, previously believed to be fished to extinction, has suddenly reappeared. Marine biologists Maria Quintero and Kevin Hoyt have come to investigate with a television producer in tow, hoping to get footage that will land them a reality TV show. The plan is to have a stand-off against a notorious illegal shark-fishing captain and then go home.

Things are not going according to plan.

There is something new in the waters of the Sea of Cortez. Something smart. Something huge. Something that has its own plans for Quintero and Hoyt.

# CHECK OUT OTHER GREAT
# DEEP SEA THRILLERS

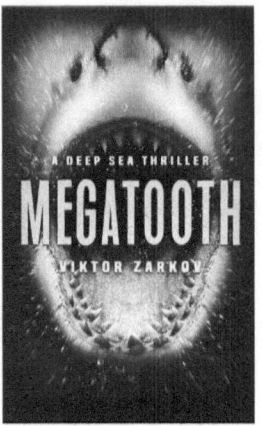

## MEGATOOTH
## by Viktor Zarkov

When the death rate of sperm whales rises dramatically, a well-respected environmental activist puts together a ragtag team to hit the high seas to investigate the matter. They suspect that the deaths are due to poachers and they are all driven by a need for justice.

Elsewhere, an experimental government vessel is enhancing deep sea mining equipment. They see one of these dead whales up close and personal...and are fairly certain that it wasn't poachers that killed it.

Both of these teams are about to discover that poachers are the least of their worries. There is something hunting the whales...

Something big
Something prehistoric.
Something terrifying.
MEGATOOTH!

## BLOOD CRUISE
## by Jake Bible

Ben Clow's plans are set. Drop off kids, pick up girlfriend, head to the marina, and hop on best friend's cruiser for a weekend of fun at sea. But Ben's happy plans are about to be changed by a tentacled horror that lurks beneath the waves.

International crime lords! Deep cover black ops agents! A ravenous, bloodsucking monster! A storm of evil and danger conspire to turn Ben Clow's vacation from a fun ocean getaway into a nightmare of a Blood Cruise!

www.ingramcontent.com/pod-product-compliance
Lightning Source LLC
Chambersburg PA
CBHW030538130626
46552CB00006B/2323